The Secret Missions of GIU Squadron 7G at RAF Grantham

WW2 Gnome Files: GIU

KIMBERLEY O'DEA-GRANT

Contents

Booklet 1: Secret Life of Squadron 7G

Booklet 2: Poison Airfield

Booklet 3: Vanishing Pilot Logs

Booklet 4: False Orders

Booklet 5: Conspiracy of the Codebreakers

Booklet 1

The Secret Life of Squadron 7G: RAF Grantham's Gnome Intelligence Unit

---

Section 1: Introduction to RAF Grantham and Squadron 7G

RAF Grantham, 1943

 The night air was thick with the low hum of propellers spinning in the distance, their rhythm a steady reminder of the war overhead. The vast expanse of RAF Grantham, one of Britain's lesser-known airbases, lay shrouded in a cloak of secrecy, its perimeter shadowed and alive with whispers of the clandestine. To most of its occupants, the base was simply another cog in the Allied war machine, training pilots and preparing sorties. But beneath the surface, there were those who knew better—those who knew of Squadron 7G.

In a hidden corner of the base, tucked away behind stacked crates and barrels, was an old, forgotten hangar. Its creaking doors and chipped paint betrayed nothing of the remarkable team that worked within. Here was the home of Squadron 7G, the gnome intelligence unit known only in whispers as "The Pocket Shadows." Led by the sharp-eyed, stoic Major Grimble Pebblewhisker, Squadron 7G operated out of sight, out of mind, and very much out of scale compared to the towering humans around them.

Though invisible to human eyes, 7G was a key player in Britain's fight against the Nazi menace. They were expert spies, equipped with enchanted tools and gnome-sized Spitfires, all modified for the unique demands of magical covert ops. With Grimble's no-nonsense command style, a reputation for cunning, and just enough old-world charm, they were ready for anything. Or, almost anything.

Inside the Hangar

"Good heavens, Fiddler, would you stop fiddling with that contraption?" Major Grimble Pebblewhisker barked, his voice a gravelly growl that matched the silver-streaked whiskers around his chin. Standing at a stout two feet, Grimble wore his officer's cap slightly askew, his uniform festooned with insignias from battles waged in miniature theaters of war. A pair of tiny, round spectacles balanced on his nose as he glared at Fiddler Twigglehook, the team's scrappy radio operator and tech expert.

"Almost got it, Major," Fiddler replied, his goggles magnifying his eyes to comedic proportions. "This little beauty here—once I adjust the signal capacity—will be able to intercept German transmissions from fifty miles out. Just think! We'll know what the sausage-slingers are up to before they even finish their first bratwurst."

"A fine bit of work, but if you don't keep it down, the humans will know what we're up to long before the sausages do," Grimble muttered, casting a wary glance toward the hangar doors.

Just then, a sharp voice chimed in from above. Willa Fernwhisk, the team's fearless reconnaissance pilot, swung down from a rafter where she'd been napping, her leather jacket and goggles giving her the look of a well-traveled adventurer. She had a spark in her eye and a sarcastic wit that could make even Grimble smile, if he was in the mood for it.

"What's the old bird fussing over now, Fiddler?" she asked, rolling her eyes as she straightened her bomber jacket.

"Only the most advanced piece of equipment to ever grace this unit," Fiddler grinned, presenting a small, enchanted box covered in knobs and levers. "The Whisper Web. With this, I'll be able to catch a whisper on the wind all the way from Berlin."

"Impressive," Willa said, raising an eyebrow. "Let's just hope it doesn't burst into flames like the last one."

"Oi, that was *one* time," Fiddler shot back. "Besides, Sparks helped build that one."

At the mention of his name, Tinker "Sparks" Bogglebright emerged from under the wing of one of their miniaturized Spitfires, covered in grease and clutching a wrench half his size. Sparks was the team's eccentric inventor, an engineer with an insatiable curiosity and a penchant for, as he put it, "constructive explosions." He had retrofitted each of the Spitfires with everything from cloaking charms to fireproof spells—just in case his modifications didn't work as planned.

"Well, it's up and running now, isn't it?" Sparks replied, pushing his goggles up and winking at Willa. "Besides, nothing ventured, nothing blown to smithereens, I always say."

Grimble cleared his throat, bringing the chatter to a halt. "As delightful as it is to hear you all bantering, I have news." His tone softened, but only just. "Intercepted a message today. Came through from HQ. It's about a potential mole here at Grantham. Seems the Nazis have their claws deeper in the base than we thought."

Silence fell over the group, the weight of the statement hanging in the air.

"Do they know who it might be?" Willa asked, her voice more serious now.

"No names, no specifics," Grimble replied, "but it's enough to make the brass nervous. They've asked us to keep our ears open—discreetly, of course. We can't afford to blow our cover, especially with the humans oblivious to our presence."

Fiddler's eyes lit up. "Well, Major, with the Whisper Web operational, I can pick up any sneaky little chat going on around here. Nothing'll get past me."

"Good," Grimble nodded, "because we're in for a long haul on this one. I want all of you on high alert. Willa, keep your eyes peeled during your flyovers. Fiddler, double-check those frequency settings, and Sparks… perhaps steer clear of anything *too* explosive until we know what we're dealing with, yes?"

Sparks saluted, though the mischievous gleam in his eye promised no guarantees. "Understood, Major."

With their orders clear, the team dispersed, each retreating to their stations. The hangar fell quiet, save for the distant thrum of planes preparing for their missions. Grimble lingered, staring at the worn blueprint on the wall that mapped RAF Grantham. His eyes traced the outlines, as if looking for any gaps, any overlooked detail that might reveal the enemy's hand.

"Just try it," he muttered under his breath. "Squadron 7G is watching."().

Section 2: Espionage and Initial Suspicions

The days following Major Grimble's orders felt like a strange calm before the storm. To the human officers of RAF Grantham, the base operated as usual: planes lifted off for recon missions, mechanics tightened bolts and fuel lines, and intelligence officers sifted through reports. But for Squadron 7G, every shadow and whispered word carried suspicion.

"Fiddler," Major Grimble called, as he stepped into the radio room, a converted supply closet where Fiddler Twigglehook had set up a command post worthy of MI6. Wires, dials, and glowing stones pulsed on the walls, and Fiddler sat at the center of it all, adjusting knobs and scribbling codes on parchment. "Any news from the Whisper Web?"

Fiddler adjusted his goggles, excitement glittering in his oversized eyes. "Just picked up something strange from the west hangar. Some of the human officers are saying 'The Raven' has spies everywhere. That's all I've heard so far."

Grimble grunted, pacing. "The Raven, eh? Sounds like a codename. Keep your ears open. If there's a leak, we'll flush it out."

Just then, the door creaked open and Willa slipped in, looking alert. "Major, you'll want to hear this," she whispered. "Just saw Flight Lieutenant Radcliffe sneaking out of the command room. He was carrying a map case—looked too full for just flight plans."

Grimble's eyes narrowed. "Radcliffe, you say?"

Willa nodded. "He's been acting strange lately. I overheard him muttering something in German last week. Could be nothing… but it could be a clue."

Grimble weighed this information carefully. Radcliffe was an unlikely suspect, but as he often reminded the team, war made traitors of surprising people. "Good work, Willa. Keep an eye on him."

That Evening: A Surveillance Operation

Under the cover of darkness, the team gathered in the cramped crawl space beneath the command room, squeezing in beside pipes and spare radio parts. Through a series of tiny holes drilled over the years, they could see the feet of the humans in the room above, pacing back and forth.

Fiddler pressed a glowing green earstone—a small enchanted device shaped like a mushroom—to the floor. His expression turned tense as he signaled the others to keep quiet.

The muffled sound of voices echoed from above.

"...and what if someone finds out?" came a man's voice, low and nervous.

"That's not our concern," replied another voice, calm and cold, unmistakably Radcliffe's. "The Raven is our contact, and we follow his orders. Next dispatch will be through the usual route."

Grimble's eyes gleamed with grim satisfaction. There it was: a confirmation that Radcliffe was involved in whatever scheme lurked under the nose of RAF Grantham's officers.

"Did you hear that?" Fiddler mouthed silently.

Grimble nodded, barely able to contain his excitement. "Our suspicions are correct. Let's get back to the hangar and regroup. If Radcliffe's involved, we may be able to trace this mole back to The Raven himself."

The team crept out, moving swiftly through the night. Back in the hangar, they gathered around a hastily cleared table, pulling out maps and notes.

"Alright," Grimble began, taking a deep breath. "We're close, but we still need more information on who The Raven is. For now, we keep this quiet. Willa, you're on Radcliffe watch. Fiddler, see if you can trace where these transmissions are going. Sparks… stay ready in case we need backup. If Radcliffe is the leak, it's only a matter of time before he makes another move."

Willa smirked, saluting with two fingers. "Aye, Major. Shadowing a human—it's practically my specialty."

Fiddler set to work immediately, adjusting the Whisper Web and tuning its frequencies, his hands moving in quick, deft motions. Sparks, meanwhile, was already fiddling with something suspiciously sparkly in his toolbox.

"Now," Grimble continued, "let's get some sleep. Tomorrow, we'll go deeper."

The Next Day: Humorous Tension and Suspicions

At dawn, the hangar was already buzzing with activity. Willa took her place near the edge of the airstrip, hidden in the tall grass with her binoculars, watching as Radcliffe strode from the officer's quarters to the command room. She couldn't resist muttering a bit of commentary as she followed his every move.

"Oy, Radcliffe, you're a shady one, aren't you?" she whispered to herself, smirking as he glanced around, looking jumpy. "Wouldn't surprise me if you had a secret stash of schnitzel somewhere in there."

Meanwhile, Fiddler was stationed in the radio room, watching the Whisper Web's dial spin, ready to intercept any suspicious communication. Sparks had set up a lookout post on a nearby ledge, fiddling with an enchanted mirror that allowed him to observe far-off areas without drawing attention.

"Got eyes on Radcliffe, Major," Willa whispered over the tiny enchanted communication stones each of the gnomes wore. "Looks like he's headed toward the south hangar now."

"Stay on him," Grimble's voice came back, terse but approving.

As the day wore on, the gnomes kept up their covert surveillance. They watched Radcliffe closely, taking note of his interactions, his odd glances, and even the occasional muttered word that seemed out of place. Yet, for all their observations, he gave away little—nothing, that is, until evening.

That Night: The First Real Lead

Just as the sun dipped below the horizon, Willa spotted Radcliffe sneaking out of his quarters, a bulky satchel slung over his shoulder. Her heart raced as she followed from a distance, keeping low and quiet. He made his way across the darkened base to a patch of trees beyond the fence, looking over his shoulder every few steps.

"Major, he's leaving the base," Willa murmured into her comm-stone. "Heading toward the treeline by the south side."

"Understood," Grimble replied. "Keep your distance, but don't lose him."

Willa slinked after him, careful not to rustle a single leaf or disturb a stone. Radcliffe paused at the edge of the forest, his gaze fixed on something in the shadows. From her position, Willa couldn't quite see what he was looking at—but then she heard it. The faint, unmistakable sound of… German.

Radcliffe was meeting someone—an unknown figure, speaking in low, hurried German. Willa's pulse quickened as she strained to catch the words, picking up phrases about "the base," "maps," and "the Raven's orders."

The meeting lasted only a few minutes, but Willa watched intently, memorizing every detail. As Radcliffe and the mysterious figure finished their conversation, Radcliffe handed over a rolled-up document, sealed with a red wax stamp.

As they parted, Willa crouched, holding her breath until the coast was clear. Only then did she turn back toward the hangar, slipping quietly into the shadows to report to Grimble and the others.

Back at the Hangar

Grimble listened, his face a mask of concentration as Willa recounted the scene. "A document, you say? And he was speaking to a German officer?" His eyes gleamed with a mixture of pride and resolve. "Well done, Willa. We have our lead. Now we just need to intercept the message before it reaches The Raven."

Fiddler was already gearing up for the task, adjusting the Whisper Web to a new frequency, hoping to pick up any transmissions from Radcliffe or his contact. Sparks, his eyes bright with excitement, began muttering about ways to "modify" a few of their gadgets for tracking purposes.

"Tomorrow night, we'll intercept that document," Grimble announced, his voice hard as stone. "It's time we let this Raven know that Squadron 7G isn't one to be trifled with."

The team exchanged glances, excitement crackling in the air. They were closing in on their target, and none of them had any intention of letting it slip away.

Section 3: The Gnomes' Magical Tools and Tactics

The following night, RAF Grantham was cloaked in shadows, with only the occasional light flickering in the distant watchtowers. In the abandoned hangar, Squadron 7G was readying themselves with an assortment of magical gadgets, each piece of equipment modified to fit their diminutive stature and enhanced for the high-stakes mission.

Inside the Hangar: Gearing Up for the Mission

Major Grimble Pebblewhisker stood at the center of the hangar, looking over a map of the base marked with strategic spots, nodding as each team member completed their preparations.

"Alright, listen up," he said, voice low but steady. "Radcliffe's got that document, and if he's delivering it tonight, we'll need to intercept it before it makes its way off base. Fiddler, you'll monitor communications to track any last-minute changes. Willa, you're in the air for an aerial watch. And Sparks…" He shot a cautious look at the engineer. "Keep your kit non-combustive, if you please."

Sparks chuckled, pulling a small, shimmering orb from his toolkit. "Nothing too volatile this time, Major. Just a Tracking Spark. I've rigged it to follow a target as long as we've marked it first with one of these."

He held up what looked like a tiny, silver dart, tipped with a needle-sharp point. The gnomes leaned in to see it closer.

"Once we tag Radcliffe, this Tracking Spark will follow him without fail," Sparks explained, grinning. "Even if he tries to toss it, it'll stick to him like a stink on a troll."

Grimble nodded approvingly. "Excellent work, Sparks. Just be careful with that—last thing we need is for it to lock onto one of us instead."

Willa, who had been readying her flight goggles, strapped them down over her eyes with a wide grin. "Just make sure you're watching, boys. I'll be swooping in and out before Radcliffe knows what's hit him."

The final device came from Fiddler, who was adjusting the Whisper Web with a series of soft, muttered incantations. The delicate wires and runes began to glow faintly, pulsing with power.

"This baby's set to pick up any frequency in a five-mile radius," Fiddler explained. "If Radcliffe so much as sneezes over a radio, we'll hear it."

Grimble couldn't help but smile. "Fine work, team. Now, let's intercept that message and find out who's been leaking our secrets to The Raven."

In the Field: Operation Interception

An hour later, Squadron 7G was deployed in the field. Grimble, Fiddler, and Sparks hid in the tall grass near the edge of the south hangar while Willa took to the skies, zipping around on her gnome-sized Spitfire. They communicated via enchanted stones, each voice crackling through with a faint shimmer.

"Major, I have eyes on Radcliffe," Willa's voice came through Grimble's comm-stone. "He's leaving the officer's quarters now, carrying the document."

"Perfect. Keep your distance and let us know when he gets close," Grimble replied, steady and calm.

As Willa shadowed Radcliffe from the air, the rest of the team moved into position. They crept quietly, slipping through shadows and taking cover behind barrels and crates, all while Fiddler monitored the Whisper Web.

"Nothing unusual on the frequencies so far," Fiddler whispered, his voice hushed. "But I'll let you know if I pick up anything."

Grimble turned to Sparks. "Now's your chance. Get that tracker on him."

Sparks grinned, taking careful aim with the silver dart. Radcliffe was just a few feet away, oblivious to the team of gnomes crouching in the shadows beside him. With a deft flick of his wrist, Sparks let the dart fly, and it struck Radcliffe's shoe with a barely audible *ting*. The Tracking Spark activated, glowing faintly as it clung to its target.

"Tagged," Sparks whispered, his grin widening. "We'll be able to follow him anywhere now."

They watched as Radcliffe made his way across the base, slipping through back paths and avoiding the guards. Grimble and the others moved in perfect silence, ducking and weaving behind cover to keep pace with him.

A Surprise Transmission

Just as Radcliffe reached the edge of the base, a faint static crackled through Fiddler's Whisper Web. He froze, straining to listen.

"Major," he whispered urgently, "we're picking something up. Sounds like he's contacting someone off-base."

Grimble leaned in, eyes narrowed. "Can you amplify it?"

Fiddler twisted the dials, his brow furrowing as he isolated the frequency. Suddenly, Radcliffe's voice came through, muffled but clear.

"...have the document. Will meet at the appointed place," Radcliffe's voice said, low and clipped. "The Raven wants this handled discreetly."

Grimble's jaw tightened. "So The Raven *is* involved. Fiddler, keep recording."

They listened as Radcliffe continued, giving the mysterious contact a set of coordinates just off-base. Grimble grinned—a rare sight, but one that meant he was planning something risky.

"Alright, team," he whispered. "He's heading to an off-base rendezvous. Willa, are you seeing anything from above?"

"Roger that, Major," Willa's voice crackled in. "I can see the meeting spot from here—looks like an old farmhouse near the woods. It's empty now, but if Radcliffe's bringing the document, he'll want privacy."

Grimble grinned again, motioning to the others. "Good. Let's intercept him there and give him a warm welcome, Squadron 7G style."

The Interception at the Farmhouse

The team reached the farmhouse a few minutes before Radcliffe, hiding themselves carefully in the rafters and shadows. Sparks rigged up a small, enchanted mirror to act as a one-way window, giving them a perfect view of Radcliffe without being seen themselves.

Finally, Radcliffe arrived, stepping inside with the document case clutched tightly under his arm. He looked around, waiting, tapping his foot impatiently.

A few tense moments passed, and then another figure appeared—a tall, thin man with slicked-back hair and a severe expression. The team froze as they recognized the emblem on his coat: a raven stitched in black thread.

"That's got to be the contact," Fiddler whispered. "We're staring at one of The Raven's men."

They watched, holding their breath, as the two men exchanged a few quiet words. Radcliffe handed over the document, and the contact slipped it inside his coat. Then he looked at Radcliffe with a smile that was far too cold for comfort.

"Your service has been noted, Lieutenant Radcliffe," the man said, his voice low and chilling.

"The Raven has plans for all of us, and once the Allies fall, you will be rewarded beyond measure."

Radcliffe merely nodded, his face pale, as if he realized too late the enormity of his betrayal.

"Let's go," Grimble murmured, signaling Sparks. "Now or never."

With a quick nod, Sparks activated one of his special tools—a small vial filled with powdered mist enchanted to cast a temporary invisibility spell. He tossed it out, and within moments, a faint, silvery fog filled the room. The humans froze, momentarily stunned as the room was plunged into shadows.

In the chaos, Grimble darted forward, snagging the document out of the contact's coat with deft hands. Sparks tossed another small device—a flash pebble—sending a bright burst of light into the room.

"Move, team!" Grimble barked.

With the humans still disoriented, the gnomes slipped out of the farmhouse, darting back into the trees. They were well away from the scene when Radcliffe's voice rang out, furious and confused, as he realized the document was gone.

Back at the Hangar: A Valuable Discovery

Safely back at RAF Grantham, the team gathered around as Grimble unrolled the document they had retrieved. Inside was a detailed map of RAF bases across Britain, each one marked with red symbols. It was a tactical plan—a list of targets that The Raven was planning to sabotage.

Grimble's eyes narrowed as he took in the document's significance. "They were planning to cripple our air defenses," he said, voice low but resolute. "And Radcliffe was feeding them everything they needed."

Willa punched the air with a victorious grin. "Well, they're not getting far with that now, are they?"

Fiddler nodded, his face grim. "The Whisper Web recorded everything. We've got all we need to stop this before it reaches The Raven."

Grimble turned to his team, pride shining in his eyes. "We've struck a blow tonight, and not a moment too soon. But remember—this is only the beginning. The Raven will be looking for us now, and he won't be taking this loss lightly."

The team shared a quiet look, a mixture of excitement and resolve. They had succeeded in their mission, but they all knew that the true battle was yet to come.

Section 4: A Dangerous Discovery

The following morning, Grimble, Willa, Fiddler, and Sparks gathered in their hidden hangar, huddled around the document they had retrieved from Radcliffe and his contact. The cool morning air filled the space as early sunlight filtered through the high, dusty windows, casting the maps and notes scattered on the table in a soft glow.

Grimble studied the document intently, his brow furrowing. "This is more than just a tactical map," he said, tapping one of the red-marked RAF bases. "They've marked locations all over Britain. If The Raven's forces are targeting each of these bases, they're planning to cripple our entire air defense."

Fiddler peered over his shoulder, adjusting his goggles. "Not just air bases, either—look here, Major." He pointed to a mark near a coastline. "This one's near the docks. They're planning something big."

Willa crossed her arms, her usual grin replaced with a serious expression. "So we're not just dealing with one mole. The Raven's got an entire network here, and if we're not careful, he'll turn the tide of this war before we even know it."

Grimble nodded, his face hardening. "Indeed. And the Germans aren't the only threat. The Raven's got allies in darker circles—forces that understand magic. We may be looking at rogue wizards or even dark creatures aiding the Nazis."

The air grew heavy with silence as the weight of the situation settled on them. But after a moment, Grimble straightened, his eyes flashing with determination. "We may be small, but we're not helpless. Let's dig into this map, see what else we can uncover, and figure out how to put a stop to this plan before it unfolds."

The First Lead: Tracing The Raven's Network

As the day wore on, the gnomes worked tirelessly, poring over the map and matching it to Fiddler's intercepted communications. By nightfall, they had pieced together a rough outline of The Raven's network. Radcliffe was only one link in a long chain; other traitors and sympathizers were embedded in airbases and command centers across Britain.

Sparks traced a red line from RAF Grantham to a base near the southern coast, his finger stopping at a small symbol: a black raven feather etched in ink. "Looks like the next target. The humans have an airbase here—small, but it's a major communications hub. If they hit it, it could cut off radio contact to half the RAF."

Grimble studied the map with grim concentration. "Then we have no choice. We intercept whatever orders come through that base and find out who's involved. If The Raven wants us to play defense, we'll give him a fight he won't forget."

Nightfall: Setting the Trap

Late that night, Squadron 7G prepared to intercept another document delivery—this time, at the south coastal airbase that Sparks had identified. The gnomes took their modified Spitfires, swooping low over the countryside to avoid detection. Flying in perfect formation, they looked like a squadron of birds to anyone who might glance skyward in the moonlight.

As they neared the coastal base, Grimble's voice crackled over the comm-stone. "Remember, team, we're aiming for stealth. If we can capture their next agent in line, we might be able to track down The Raven's full network. Fiddler, are you set to intercept?"

"Roger that, Major," Fiddler replied. He had set up the Whisper Web in one of the nearby hangars, tuning into the base's communication frequency. "I'll let you know the moment they make contact."

The night stretched on in tense silence. The only sounds were the faint rustling of wind and the occasional far-off buzz of an engine as a human aircraft returned from its mission. Willa took position near the airstrip, crouched in the shadows, while Sparks and Grimble lay hidden just outside the command center.

Finally, Fiddler's voice came through the comm-stone. "Major, I've got something. It's our friend Radcliffe, and he's not alone. They're headed your way now, to the comms room."

Infiltration of the Comms Room

Grimble and Sparks slipped through a ventilation shaft into the comms room, cloaked by a silencing spell. They crouched behind a filing cabinet, watching as Radcliffe entered, accompanied by a tall figure cloaked in black. Unlike the previous contact, this one's presence sent a chill down Grimble's spine—there was something distinctly unnatural about him.

As the two humans began to speak in low voices, Grimble activated his Whisper Web, amplifying their conversation.

"It's imperative that this document reaches The Raven tonight," the tall figure said, his voice eerily smooth. "Failure is not an option, Radcliffe. If you fail us again, the consequences will be… unpleasant."

Radcliffe swallowed hard, his face pale. "Understood, sir. I'll deliver it myself."

The man handed over a rolled document sealed with black wax, a raven feather pressed into the stamp. Radcliffe took it, glancing nervously toward the door before pocketing the message.

Sparks' eyes gleamed as he held up another of his enchanted tracking darts, ready to strike as soon as Radcliffe turned his back. But just as Sparks prepared to throw it, the tall man stiffened, his head tilting slightly as if he had sensed their presence.

Grimble held his breath, motioning for Sparks to stay still. The man's gaze scanned the room, his eyes narrowing as they passed over their hiding spot.

"Something's wrong," he murmured, his voice laced with suspicion. "We're not alone here."

Before the gnomes could react, the man flicked his wrist, muttering a spell in a language neither Grimble nor Sparks recognized. Shadows began to swirl around him, taking on the shapes of clawed hands reaching toward their hiding place.

"Run!" Grimble whispered, grabbing Sparks and darting out from behind the cabinet.

They barely escaped the room as the shadows closed in, slipping back into the ventilation shaft and scurrying through the narrow tunnels toward the safety of the base's outer perimeter.

Back at the Hangar: Grim News

When they regrouped back at the hangar, the team was visibly shaken. Grimble took a deep breath, gathering his composure as he looked around at his team.

"That man was no ordinary contact," Grimble said, his voice grave. "Whatever he is, he's not just a sympathizer. I'd wager he's working with dark forces, possibly even using forbidden magic. If The Raven has allies like that in his ranks, we're dealing with far more than human traitors."

Willa's face was set in a determined scowl. "If they're bringing dark magic into this war, then we'll just have to get creative with our own tactics, won't we?"

Grimble nodded, his eyes hardening. "We'll need to alert our allies. The humans can't know, but I know of a few wizards loyal to the Allies who may be able to help us counter this threat. Fiddler, send a coded message to the Allied Magical Division. Tell them it's urgent."

Fiddler nodded, immediately setting to work, his fingers flying over the dials as he tuned the Whisper Web to a secure frequency.

As they waited, Sparks began tinkering with a new device, muttering to himself as he reinforced its casing with layers of enchanted metal. "If they want a fight, they'll get one. And I'll make sure we have a few surprises waiting for them."

Grimble watched his team, a sense of pride swelling within him. They had all faced danger before, but this was different. They were up against an enemy that wielded powers beyond their understanding, yet none of them were backing down.

"We may be small, but we're far from defenseless," Grimble said quietly. "And if The Raven thinks he can push us into a corner, he's got another thing coming."

Section 5: Aerial Dogfight with Dark Forces

RAF Grantham, Midnight

The air was crisp and still, broken only by the distant rumble of engines as the night's patrol returned to base. But in the shadows of the hidden hangar, Squadron 7G prepared for battle. They had just received an urgent message through the Whisper Web: enemy forces were en route, likely to launch a coordinated strike at several RAF bases. And, alarmingly, some of these enemies were rumored to be enhanced with dark magic.

"We've got hostile flyers coming in from the southeast," Fiddler reported, his voice tense as he tuned the Whisper Web to a secure frequency. "Looks like they're headed right for us, Major."

Grimble Pebblewhisker, calm but grim, adjusted his tiny flight cap. "If they're expecting an easy target, they're in for a surprise. Willa, you're in the lead. Fiddler, keep monitoring any signals coming our way. Sparks, make sure those cloaking charms are in place. This time, we're the hunters."

The team climbed into their enchanted mini-Spitfires, each plane custom-fitted with magical charms and modifications that made them formidable despite their small size. They taxied out of the hangar in single file, and one by one, took to the air. Tiny engines roared to life, sending the gnomes soaring up, silhouetted briefly against the pale light of the moon.

The Enemy Approaches

As they gained altitude, Willa took point, peering ahead through her enchanted goggles. The landscape below stretched dark and vast, but she spotted the enemy squadron—a line of tiny black dots weaving through the sky, eerie and silent.

"Eyes on them, Major," she said over the comm-stone. "Looks like… six enemy craft, at least two of them carrying dark energy signatures. They've got enchanted weaponry, too."

Grimble's voice crackled through her headset. "Stay sharp, Willa. No solo heroics. We work as a team."

"Aye, Major," she replied, her tone calm but tinged with a spark of excitement.

Willa signaled the others as they closed the distance, angling their planes to flank the enemy formation. She could feel the hum of magic within her Spitfire as she engaged the charms Sparks had rigged into the wings. The planes were fast, maneuverable, and enchanted with cloaking spells that allowed them to blend into the night sky—a significant advantage against the shadowy enemy forces.

They swooped down, engines whirring quietly, until they were nearly upon the enemy squadron. But as they prepared to strike, one of the enemy planes broke formation, spiraling back and releasing a strange, shimmering mist into the sky.

"Cloaking magic," Sparks muttered over the comm. "They're trying to hide."

"Let's show them how it's done," Grimble replied. "Willa, take them in fast!"

The Dogfight Begins

Willa dived first, her tiny Spitfire racing through the mist with ease, her charms cutting through the enemy's magic. She fired off a burst of energy from her enchanted pulse blaster, a streak of green light slicing through the air and landing a glancing blow on the lead enemy plane. It spiraled slightly, regaining control just in time to avoid plummeting from the sky.

"Direct hit!" Willa crowed. But her victory was short-lived.

The enemy leader—a pilot clad in dark leather with an insignia of a raven feather on his shoulder—threw a hand out, casting a shadowy spell that wrapped around Willa's plane like a net.

"Major! I'm caught!" Willa's voice was tense, her Spitfire struggling as the dark magic dragged it downward. She fought the controls, teeth clenched as the dark tendrils tightened.

"Hold on, Willa! Sparks, you're up," Grimble barked.

Sparks dove in from above, pulling out a small orb from his cockpit and launching it toward the dark spell. The orb exploded on contact, releasing a flash of brilliant light that shattered the shadowy tendrils holding Willa's plane.

"Gotcha free, Willa!" Sparks whooped. "Now let's see if they like a bit of their own medicine."

Willa regained control, yanking her Spitfire back into position and spinning around to flank the enemy leader, who glared at her through the darkness. She returned the glare, her eyes alight with defiance.

Magical Weapons and Tactical Maneuvers

The battle escalated. Enemy gnomes wielded enchanted cannons that spat bursts of dark energy, and some even cast spells that sent shimmering, spectral hands clawing at the RAF planes, trying to rip the gnomes from the cockpits. But Squadron 7G was prepared.

"Evasive maneuvers!" Grimble ordered, diving sharply to avoid a blast of dark energy that narrowly missed him. He circled back, positioning himself behind one of the enemy gnomes and firing a quick series of blaster pulses. The enemy plane jolted, smoke billowing from the engine as it spiraled out of control.

Meanwhile, Fiddler had his hands full, monitoring enemy communications through the Whisper Web while trying to keep track of the fast-paced dogfight. "Major, they're calling for backup. I'm picking up an encrypted message—looks like The Raven's forces are spread out over the southeast coast."

"Copy that," Grimble replied. "Let's finish up here quickly before we're overrun."

Sparks was in his element, diving and twisting through the sky as he deployed a series of smoke pellets, creating clouds of thick, magical fog that disoriented the enemy planes. He fired off a modified blaster shot that exploded into a burst of sparks, temporarily blinding two enemy gnomes who veered off course.

"Ha! Take that, you sorry lot!" Sparks shouted, his laughter crackling over the comm-stone.

Willa, meanwhile, took advantage of the chaos, darting back into the fray with her Spitfire's pulse blasters at full power. She focused on the enemy leader, who was circling back for another attack, his dark magic swirling around him like a storm. She locked onto him, firing a precise burst of energy that landed squarely on his wing.

The enemy leader's plane lurched, and for a moment, he looked stunned, his dark magic flickering and fading.

A Narrow Escape

As the battle raged on, the enemy forces began to falter. One by one, the gnomes of Squadron 7G forced the dark flyers to retreat, each one disappearing into the night like vanishing shadows. Finally, only the enemy leader remained, his damaged plane trailing smoke as he tried to escape.

But Grimble wasn't about to let him slip away. He swooped in close, angling his plane just above the leader's cockpit. "This is your one chance," Grimble's voice crackled over the comm-stone, loud enough for the enemy pilot to hear. "Call off your attacks, or we'll make sure you never see another nightfall."

The leader's eyes narrowed, but he gave a slow nod, casting one last, venomous glance at Grimble before veering off, disappearing into the blackness.

"Good riddance," Grimble muttered, his heart still pounding as he rejoined his team. "That was a message, alright—from The Raven himself."

Back at the Hangar: The Aftermath

Back on the ground, Squadron 7G regrouped in the hangar, their faces a mix of triumph and exhaustion. Willa's plane had a scorched wing, and Sparks was missing one of his smoke launchers, but the team was intact.

Grimble took a steadying breath as he addressed the others. "We faced dark magic out there, and we held our own. But The Raven knows we're a threat now, and he won't be underestimating us again."

Fiddler nodded, his eyes hard. "That's right. I intercepted a transmission during the fight—The Raven's planning something big, and soon. The encrypted code suggests a coordinated strike on three bases, all within the week."

"Then we need to be ready," Grimble said firmly. "We'll need every trick, every charm, and every ounce of courage we've got."

Sparks grinned, holding up a new, glinting gadget he had cobbled together in the heat of battle. "I think we can manage that, Major."

As the first light of dawn began to brighten the sky, Squadron 7G stood together in silent determination. They had won a battle, but the war against The Raven was only just beginning.

Section 6: A Deeper Look at "The Raven"

RAF Grantham Hangar, Dawn

After the grueling dogfight, the members of Squadron 7G had retreated to their makeshift command center in the hidden hangar. Worn and weary but undeterred, the team pored over intercepted transmissions and new intelligence they'd pieced together from the night's battle. The dark magic, the enemy pilots, and the relentless pursuit all pointed to one terrifying conclusion: The Raven was preparing something massive.

Grimble Pebblewhisker sat at the head of the table, his gaze fixed on the map spread before him. A network of red threads and marked locations snaked across it, each representing a site connected to The Raven's agents. The entire southeast coast, from Grantham down to Dover, was covered with pins, and their impact was becoming chillingly clear.

Fiddler traced one of the threads with his finger, his brow furrowed. "Based on these coordinates, we've got three major bases he's targeting in the next week. And if he sabotages them, he'll create a corridor straight into London."

Willa's eyes widened as she looked over Fiddler's shoulder. "You're saying he'd have a path open for an invasion?"

Fiddler nodded grimly. "Or at least, a way to launch a powerful attack with dark forces. Imagine it—creatures, rogue wizards, enchanted weapons. If he gets that corridor, he could deal a blow to London itself."

Sparks, ever the tinkerer, was distractedly adjusting one of his gadgets but listened closely. "So, we're talking about an invasion backed by dark magic? Blimey. That's no ordinary battle. That's... well, that's doom on our doorstep."

Grimble's voice cut through the tension. "Not if we stop him first." He pointed to a mark on the map—a small, unnamed spot in the countryside south of Grantham. "This location is key. It's an old farmhouse, the one where Radcliffe met his contact. If we go there, we might find clues to the full scope of The Raven's plans."

A Hidden Farmhouse: The Secrets Within

Later that night, Squadron 7G prepared for a ground mission to investigate the farmhouse. They armed themselves with cloaking charms, enchanted lanterns, and one of Sparks' latest inventions—a spell-breaking powder designed to neutralize dark magic.

The gnomes moved swiftly through the countryside, staying hidden in the shadows of the tall grass. The farmhouse lay abandoned, silhouetted against the moonlight. Its windows were boarded, its walls weathered, but it pulsed with a strange, dark energy that made the gnomes' skin prickle.

Grimble signaled for silence as they approached, his voice barely a whisper. "Remember, we're looking for any documents, magical artifacts—anything that might link The Raven to his network."

They split into pairs. Willa and Sparks took the ground floor, while Grimble and Fiddler made their way to the upper rooms. The house creaked underfoot, and the air was thick with the scent of must and faintly charred wood, as if someone had burned something important recently.

In the main room, Willa and Sparks discovered an old, dusty chest, locked and covered in strange symbols.

"What do you reckon, Sparks? Think you can open it?" Willa asked, her eyes gleaming with excitement.

Sparks grinned, pulling out a small vial of spell-breaking powder. "Oh, I reckon I can do more than open it."

He sprinkled the powder over the chest, murmuring a few words of activation. The symbols on the chest flickered, then faded, and with a soft click, the lock opened. Inside was a stack of documents written in German, as well as a small black book with a raven embossed on the cover.

Willa's eyes widened. "The Raven's codebook! This could give us the names of every agent he has in Britain."

Sparks nodded, carefully slipping the book into his pouch. "Let's get this to the Major. I have a feeling this is exactly what we need."

The Raven's Codebook: A Dark Revelation

Back at the hangar, Grimble examined the codebook, his face serious. Fiddler set up his Whisper Web, translating the contents while Willa and Sparks looked on. The pages revealed names, locations, and encoded orders for sabotage across Britain.

Grimble ran a finger down the list of names, his expression darkening as he read aloud. "These are high-ranking officers, government officials… and wizards. The Raven's corrupted half of London's magical circles. He's got rogue wizards aiding him from the inside."

Fiddler looked up from the Whisper Web, his face pale. "One of these orders here—it's scheduled for the next full moon. He's coordinating a dark ritual. If he pulls it off, he'll unleash enough dark energy to devastate every RAF base within fifty miles."

Sparks exhaled sharply, his fists clenching. "A ritual of that scale? That's forbidden magic! If he succeeds, it could tear a hole in the fabric of our world!"

Grimble's eyes flashed with anger, but he remained composed. "Then we stop him, here and now. We've got a few days until the full moon. We'll need to intercept his forces, disrupt the ritual, and neutralize his network before he can activate it."

Willa placed a reassuring hand on Fiddler's shoulder. "You know we're with you, Major. We'll fight till the last feather if we have to."

Grimble nodded, his gaze moving over each of his team with steely determination. "Good. Because our next move will be our biggest yet. Tomorrow, we set a trap for The Raven. He's cast his shadow far enough. Now, it's time we bring him into the light."

Preparing for the Final Showdown

The night was alive with quiet activity as Squadron 7G prepared for what they knew would be a decisive battle. Sparks worked late, modifying the Spitfires with extra shielding spells and fitting each plane with anti-dark-magic amulets he had forged from enchanted iron. Fiddler fine-tuned the Whisper Web, amplifying its range to catch every message from The Raven's network.

In the quiet moments, the team shared glances, each one understanding the stakes. They had fought The Raven's forces before, but this was different. They would be facing rogue wizards, dark creatures, and forces that twisted magic into shadows. Yet none of them faltered.

Grimble finally called them together as dawn broke, his voice steady as he addressed them. "This is it, Squadron 7G. We're facing one of the darkest forces Britain has ever known, but we're not alone. We've got skill, courage, and each other. Tonight, we'll show The Raven that not even his shadows can stand against the light of this team."

Sparks gave a firm nod, clutching one of his new amulets. "Let's bring him down, Major."

With that, the team dispersed, each one going to their posts, ready to face the dawn with their heads held high. The final battle against The Raven was coming, and Squadron 7G would be there to meet it.

Section 7: A Secret Meeting with Allied Wizards

RAF Grantham, Midnight

The old clock in the hangar struck midnight, its chimes echoing softly through the stillness. But tonight, the calm was anything but ordinary. Squadron 7G, led by Major Grimble Pebblewhisker, was headed for a covert meeting in the nearby woods—one that could turn the tide of their fight against The Raven.

Grimble and his team moved under the cover of darkness, staying close to the base's edge and making their way toward the gathering spot. Each carried small enchanted lanterns, their soft blue light flickering in sync, a signal to the allies they hoped would be waiting.

After a short walk, the woods opened into a clearing illuminated by the soft glow of enchanted torches. There, gathered in a half-circle, stood a small but distinguished group of figures. Dressed in robes of varying shades, some wore the insignias of the Allied Magical Division, while others bore the faint markings of forest druids or the quiet demeanor of hedge wizards.

At the center of the group stood **Master Elowen Cragsparrow**, one of the senior wizards in the Allied magical network. With his long silver beard and a steady gaze that seemed to pierce through the night, he turned to Grimble as they approached, nodding in solemn greeting.

"Major Pebblewhisker," Elowen said in a voice that seemed to resonate with the trees themselves. "I trust your team is prepared?"

Grimble straightened, his voice steady. "We are, Master Elowen. But we're up against dark forces— The Raven's network is deep, and he's using forbidden magic. We've come to seek your aid."

Elowen's expression darkened. "We've been monitoring The Raven's activities. We know he's been gathering rogue wizards and creatures willing to betray our kind. If he succeeds in this ritual, he could open a gateway for his dark allies."

Willa frowned, crossing her arms. "If it's that bad, then we're running out of time, aren't we?"

Elowen nodded gravely. "Indeed. But we have a plan to counter his magic. It will require immense energy and precise timing. We'll need your help to execute it."

The Plan: Counteracting The Raven's Ritual

Elowen gestured toward a small satchel that one of the druids had brought forward. Inside were fragments of crystals, each one glowing faintly with a soft, silver light.

"These are nullifying crystals," Elowen explained. "They're charged to break dark spells, but they have limited range. If you place them in key spots around the ritual site, they'll disrupt the flow of magic. If everything goes right, it will force The Raven's spell to collapse."

Fiddler's eyes lit up as he examined the crystals. "If we can get close enough to plant these, it'll give us a chance to stop the ritual without facing the full brunt of The Raven's magic."

Grimble studied the crystals, nodding thoughtfully. "A clever plan. And what of The Raven's forces? His allies will certainly be guarding the area."

"We'll handle that," replied another wizard, a young woman with deep green robes and a calm, determined face. "Our team will draw away his guards and intercept any reinforcements. You'll have to be swift, though. If his ritual reaches its peak, even these crystals may not be enough to stop it."

Sparks glanced at Grimble, his face serious. "I can rig our Spitfires to carry these crystals. If we drop them around the ritual site in a wide arc, it'll give us the best shot at cutting off his magic."

Willa grinned, her eyes gleaming with a mix of excitement and determination. "Then let's do it. We've faced worse odds, haven't we?"

Elowen placed a hand on Grimble's shoulder, his voice lowering. "Remember, Major, this ritual has drawn in powerful, malevolent forces. Be wary. They'll have defenses even our magic may not breach."

Grimble nodded. "We understand. And we're ready. If The Raven thinks he can bring dark forces to Britain's shores, he'll find he's miscalculated."

The Walk Back: Final Preparations

The meeting concluded, and Squadron 7G made their way back to the base. There was an unspoken tension in the air; each gnome was lost in their thoughts, each knowing that the battle ahead would be like nothing they'd faced before.

As they neared the hangar, Grimble paused, turning to address his team. "This is it. We're about to face The Raven and his allies head-on. But remember, we're not just fighting for ourselves. We're fighting to protect everyone who calls this island home."

Fiddler gave a firm nod, his usual playfulness replaced with a look of steely resolve. "We'll do what we have to, Major."

Willa flashed a confident smile. "This Raven's going to wish he'd stuck to cawing in trees when we're through with him."

Sparks gave them all a thumbs-up, holding up one of the crystals. "Then let's get to work. I've got some spells to reinforce, and these beauties to fit into our planes."

With a nod, Grimble led them back to the hangar, where each gnome took up their tasks. Sparks began attaching the nullifying crystals to their Spitfires, carefully setting each one in place to ensure they would be easy to release during their mission. Fiddler double-checked the Whisper Web for any last-minute intel, while Willa calibrated her goggles, her mind racing with the maneuvers she'd need to pull off.

As dawn approached, their preparations were complete. Squadron 7G stood together one last time, a quiet but fierce determination in each of their eyes.

"We'll be ready, Major," Willa said, her voice filled with certainty.

Grimble looked at each of his team members, pride and respect filling his heart. "Then let's go. Tonight, we finish this."

Section 8: The Final Showdown at RAF Grantham

RAF Grantham, Twilight

The sun dipped below the horizon, casting long shadows over the base as the night began to fall. RAF Grantham was quiet, every soldier and pilot oblivious to the storm about to unfold in their midst. But in the hidden hangar, Squadron 7G was anything but calm. This was the night they would face The Raven.

Sparks gave the last crystal a final twist, securing it in Willa's Spitfire. He stepped back, wiping his hands and giving her a firm nod. "All set, Willa. These crystals are ready to disrupt even the nastiest dark magic. Just get them close enough to the ritual site, and they'll do their job."

Grimble called the team to attention. "Alright, everyone. We've got one shot to pull this off. The Raven's ritual will be underway shortly, and we need to break the spell before it reaches its full power. Remember, we're dealing with dark forces here—stay sharp and stick to the plan."

Each of them nodded, gripping their comm-stones tightly. They climbed into their Spitfires, preparing to lift off. The modified planes hummed with a potent blend of magical energy and old-fashioned gnome ingenuity, ready to take on whatever The Raven had in store.

Grimble's voice crackled over the comm-stone. "Squadron 7G, prepare for takeoff."

One by one, the tiny Spitfires taxied out of the hangar, lining up on the shadowed airstrip. In a burst of coordinated power, they lifted off, soaring into the darkening sky. Below them, RAF Grantham shrank to a patchwork of lights and shadows, but the gnomes' attention was fixed on the forest to the south, where The Raven's ritual was rumored to be underway.

Approaching the Ritual Site

As they neared the forest, an unnatural glow pulsed from within the trees, casting an eerie light that flickered like fire and shadow. The air grew thick, almost electric, as the ritual's dark energy radiated outward. It was a force unlike any Squadron 7G had ever felt—a mixture of ancient magic and malignant intent, one that chilled them to the bone.

Willa was the first to spot the ritual site, her goggles zeroing in on a stone circle surrounded by shadowy figures. At the center stood The Raven himself, a tall figure draped in black, his eyes glowing with an unholy light as he chanted an incantation that filled the air with a terrible resonance.

"Eyes on the target," Willa reported. "The Raven's at the center of the ritual. We'll need to plant these crystals close to him to break the spell."

Grimble's voice came through, steady but tense. "We'll create a distraction. Sparks, you're with me. Fiddler, stay back and monitor the ritual's energy. Willa, get in as close as you can and drop those crystals."

"Aye, Major," Willa replied, gripping the controls tightly. "Let's show this raven how gnomes handle a fight."

The Battle Begins

As the gnomes swooped down, The Raven looked up, his face twisting into a sneer. He raised a hand, muttering an incantation, and from the shadows emerged dark creatures—spectral hounds with glowing red eyes, circling the ritual site like twisted sentries.

"Those are shadow hounds!" Fiddler shouted over the comm-stone. "They're bred to hunt by scent, and they'll track us through any cloaking magic."

"Then we'll just have to outmaneuver them," Grimble replied, his voice firm. "Squadron 7G, engage!"

With a sudden burst of speed, Willa dived toward the stone circle, dropping her first crystal. It landed near the edge of the ritual, pulsing with a soft, silver glow. The shadows around it recoiled, and a faint tremor rippled through the dark energy as it began to destabilize.

The Raven's face twisted in fury, and he cast a hand outward, summoning more shadow hounds that sprinted after Willa, their spectral forms closing in on her plane. Willa twisted sharply, dodging left and right as the hounds lunged, their jaws snapping just inches from her wings.

"Willa, bank left—I'll take them!" Sparks shouted, releasing one of his enchanted flare bombs. The bomb exploded in a burst of blinding light, and the shadow hounds howled as the magic burned them, forcing them to retreat momentarily.

Willa grinned. "Thanks, Sparks! Going in for another drop!"

Breaking the Ritual

As the crystals fell, each one disrupted the ritual's magic, sending ripples through the spell that The

Raven fought to keep stable. Grimble and Sparks circled above, firing enchanted bursts that crackled with protective magic, holding off the shadow hounds and drawing fire from the wizards guarding the perimeter.

The Raven raised his hands, dark energy coiling around him as he summoned an enormous wave of shadow. It billowed outward, swallowing the light and reaching hungrily toward the gnomes' planes.

"Brace yourselves!" Grimble shouted. "Willa, plant the last crystal!"

Willa dived, racing toward the center of the ritual, her fingers gripping the last nullifying crystal. She aimed carefully, her eyes fixed on the heart of the ritual where The Raven stood. In one swift motion, she released the crystal, watching as it arced through the air and landed at The Raven's feet.

For a moment, everything went still. The Raven's eyes widened as the crystal pulsed, its energy flaring and rippling through the ritual circle, breaking the lines of magic and scattering the symbols in a flash of silver light.

"No!" The Raven's voice echoed through the clearing, filled with rage and desperation. He tried to recast the spell, but the magic slipped from his grasp, unraveling as the crystals disrupted the dark energy at its core.

The ground shook, and the shadows around him began to writhe and dissipate, leaving the stone circle bathed in the soft glow of the nullifying crystals.

A Final Stand

But The Raven wasn't done. He turned his gaze to Squadron 7G, his eyes blazing with hatred. Raising his hand, he gathered the last of his energy into a concentrated bolt of dark magic, aiming it straight at Grimble.

Grimble saw the attack coming, but before he could react, Willa dived between him and The Raven, intercepting the blast. The dark energy hit her plane, sending it spiraling out of control, flames licking at her wings.

"Willa!" Sparks shouted, horror in his voice.

But Willa's voice crackled over the comm-stone, steady despite the chaos. "I'm alright! Just… a little singed. Keep going, finish him off!"

Grimble gritted his teeth, anger and determination burning in his eyes. He flew directly toward The Raven, dodging bursts of shadow as he closed in. Sparks joined him, firing one of his last enchanted rounds, which exploded in a brilliant burst, sending The Raven staggering back.

With one final push, Grimble unleashed a volley of enchanted blaster fire, each shot striking with the force of a gnome's courage and grit. The Raven stumbled, his dark magic weakening as the spells hit him, shattering his control.

Finally, with a roar of defiance, The Raven fell to his knees, the last of his magic dissipating in the air. The shadows around him faded, leaving the stone circle empty, stripped of its dark power.

Victory at Dawn

As the first light of dawn broke over the trees, Squadron 7G regrouped in the clearing, their Spitfires battered but intact. Willa's plane had lost a wingtip, and Sparks' engine was trailing smoke, but they were alive. And they had won.

Grimble climbed from his plane, his gaze fixed on the now-empty circle, his expression somber. "The Raven's darkness is broken, but there will be others like him. We'll need to stay vigilant."

Willa clapped him on the shoulder, her face smudged with soot but her eyes bright. "And we will. Together."

Fiddler looked over at Sparks, grinning. "We make a pretty good team, don't we?"

Sparks smirked, holding up one of his last flare bombs. "Best in the RAF, if you ask me."

The team shared a quiet, proud smile as they watched the sun rise. They knew that there would be more battles, more enemies lurking in the shadows. But with each other, they were ready to face whatever lay ahead.

Section 9: Epilogue and Reflections

RAF Grantham, Dawn

As the sun rose over RAF Grantham, the base was quiet, still unaware of the battle that had raged in the shadows. Squadron 7G, weary and worn, landed their Spitfires in the hidden hangar. They moved with a shared silence, each member feeling the weight of the night's events in their bones. But beneath the exhaustion was a fierce pride—they had faced The Raven's dark forces, and they had won.

Inside the hangar, the team carefully tended to their planes, checking for damages and dusting off remnants of the battle. Sparks was already at work on Willa's singed wingtip, muttering as he reattached bolts and applied a fresh layer of enchanted paint.

"Nearly lost a wing there, didn't you, Willa?" he said with a grin, his usual humor returning now that the danger had passed.

Willa laughed, brushing a bit of soot from her jacket. "Nothing I couldn't handle. Besides, someone had to keep Grimble from getting himself turned into a gnome kebab."

Grimble looked up from where he was cleaning his blaster, a rare smile tugging at the corners of his mouth. "If I recall, I had the situation under control," he said, his voice tinged with warmth. "But you did well, all of you. The Raven was a formidable enemy, and we defeated him as a team."

Fiddler looked around at his friends, a thoughtful expression on his face. "Do you think it's really over, Major? The Raven's gone, but he had allies. And who knows how many sympathizers are still out there?"

Grimble nodded, his face growing serious. "You're right, Fiddler. This may be the end of The Raven's plans, but there will always be others drawn to the darkness. We may be small, but we're the line between that darkness and the people we've sworn to protect."

The others fell silent, each reflecting on the battles they had fought and the challenges they would continue to face. But the quiet was one of understanding, not fear—they had chosen this fight, and they would continue it as long as there were shadows to face.

A Quiet Celebration

After repairing their planes, the team settled around a small table in the hangar, sharing a humble breakfast of tea and biscuits. Sparks had managed to find a dusty tin of chocolates, which he passed around with a grin.

"To victories big and small," he said, raising a biscuit in a mock toast. "And to the finest gnome squadron this side of Britain."

They all clinked their biscuits together, laughing as they recounted stories from the night's battle, teasing each other over near-misses and daring maneuvers. For a few moments, the weight of the world lifted, replaced by the warmth of friendship and the relief of survival.

Looking to the Future

As the sun climbed higher, the team knew it was time to rest, but each of them felt the spark of adventure still flickering in their hearts.

Grimble stood, looking out at the sky, his voice quiet but filled with resolve. "Remember, our duty doesn't end here. RAF Grantham may not know of us, but they depend on us all the same. And when the next threat comes, we'll be ready."

Willa grinned, adjusting her goggles. "As long as you're leading us, Major, there's no place I'd rather be."

Sparks and Fiddler echoed her sentiment, each nodding with a determination that matched their leader's. They knew that as long as Squadron 7G was together, there was no enemy they couldn't face.

Grimble looked around at his team, his expression softening as he saw the loyalty and bravery in each of their faces. "Then let's rest, recharge, and be ready for whatever comes next. Because as long as there are shadows to be cleared, Squadron 7G will be there to light the way."

And with that, the team gathered their gear, each one holding their head high as they left the hangar. They were tired, yes, but more than that, they were ready. Ready for the battles yet to come, the enemies they had yet to meet, and the skies that would always be theirs to protect.

The End.

Booklet 2

Poisoned Airfield: The Secret Operation of Squadron 7G

Section 1: The Mystery Begins

RAF Grantham, England - March 1943

The night sky stretched dark and endless over RAF  Grantham, the stars barely piercing the heavy mist that settled over the base. By all appearances, it was a night like any other at the airfield: mechanics checked engines, pilots prepared for early morning sorties, and the deep hum of aircraft engines rumbled through the cold air. But tonight, something was wrong.

Sergeant Colin Baird, one of the senior mechanics, stood just outside Hangar 4, hunched over a thermos of tea that was doing little to keep him warm. He'd felt a strange chill all night, and no amount of tea seemed to help. Just as he was considering a break, a voice shouted from inside the hangar.

"Sergeant! You'd better get in here—quick!"

The urgency in the voice jolted Colin from his thoughts, and he rushed inside. His heart dropped as he saw two young mechanics, both slumped against the fuselage of the aircraft they'd been servicing, their faces pale and their hands shaking. Nearby, another mechanic knelt over them, looking frantic.

"What happened here?" Colin demanded, his voice sharp.

The mechanic shook his head, clearly at a loss. "They were fine just minutes ago. We'd just finished tightening up the landing gear. Then, all of a sudden, they start feeling faint and couldn't hold their tools steady. It's like... like something hit them."

Colin's face darkened as he took in the scene. This wasn't the first time he'd seen mechanics fall ill after working on these particular aircraft. Just last week, another group had reported sudden nausea and dizziness after an overnight shift. They'd all blamed it on lack of sleep, but now... now it was looking like something far more serious.

"I'll report it to the CO," Colin said grimly. "But keep this quiet for now. Last thing we need is a panic spreading across the base."

As he made his way toward the command building, Colin couldn't shake the uneasy feeling that crept over him. Sabotage had always been a distant worry—something that happened at other bases, to other people. But this time, it felt like the threat had come home to Grantham.

The Gnomes of Squadron 7G

Meanwhile, in a small, hidden corner of the base that no human knew existed, another team was already on high alert. Squadron 7G, RAF Grantham's covert gnome intelligence unit, was headquartered in an abandoned storage shed near the airfield, their hangar hidden from human eyes by a clever spell woven years ago.

Major Grimble Pebblewhisker, the leader of the squadron, leaned over a tiny table cluttered with maps, intel reports, and strange gadgets. Standing just over eight inches tall, he wore his officer's cap slightly askew, his grizzled whiskers giving him an air of serious determination. His eyes narrowed as he studied the report in front of him.

"Major, I've picked up a strange transmission," Fiddler Twigglehook said, adjusting the dials on his miniature radio set. Fiddler, the team's tech expert, was hunched over the Whisper Web—a web of enchanted radio wires that let him eavesdrop on human communications.

Grimble looked up, brow furrowing. "What's it say?"

"It's from the humans' command center," Fiddler replied. "Seems some of the mechanics have fallen ill. Not sure why yet, but word is, they were all working on the same set of aircraft."

Grimble grunted, a thoughtful gleam in his eye. "Ill, you say? That could be more than bad luck. Might even be sabotage."

Just then, the hangar doors opened, and Willa Fernwhisk stepped inside, her pilot goggles pushed up on her head and her jacket dusted with engine grease. She had just come back from a reconnaissance flight, and her keen eyes and quick thinking made her the perfect scout.

"Looks like there's a bit of a stir at the main hangar, Major," she said. "Some of the mechanics were muttering about sickness spreading through the crew. Something about poisoned food?"

Grimble stroked his whiskers thoughtfully. "Food poisoning, eh? A likely excuse, but too convenient for my liking. If there's a threat in those aircraft, we need to know what it is—and fast."

He turned to Fiddler and Sparks, who was busy tinkering with a set of tools in the corner, his fingers stained with oil. "Sparks, I want you to assemble a field inspection kit. If this is sabotage, it could be hidden in the aircraft's metal, and we'll need a way to detect it."

Sparks, the team's inventive engineer, grinned and gave a brisk salute. "On it, Major. I've got just the thing. A bit of enchanted powder and a sensitivity spell—I'll whip up a kit that'll detect anything unusual in that metal."

Grimble nodded, his expression hardening. "Good. And Willa, I'll need you on standby. We may need your help if things go south."

Willa flashed him a confident grin. "You can count on me, Major."

As the gnomes prepared for their covert inspection, Grimble felt a familiar thrill settle in his bones. This wasn't their first mission, but every one felt like the most important. Squadron 7G was used to operating in the shadows, keeping the base safe from threats the humans never even knew existed. And this time, it seemed, was no different.

Incognito Inspection

An hour later, the gnomes made their way across the base, slipping between crates and hiding behind barrels as they approached Hangar 4. Grimble moved with practiced stealth, his small size making it easy to avoid detection. He signaled for Sparks to set up his inspection kit near the affected aircraft, a sturdy bomber with its metal gleaming faintly in the dim light.

Sparks knelt beside the landing gear, his hands deftly applying a dusting of enchanted powder across the metal. Almost immediately, the powder reacted, glowing a faint green—a telltale sign of something suspicious.

"Major, we've got something here," Sparks whispered, holding up the now-green powder. "This isn't standard corrosion—it's something else, something... toxic."

Grimble's expression turned grim. "A poison?"

"Most likely," Sparks replied. "But it's subtle, like it's embedded in the metal itself. If I had to guess, I'd say it's designed to release when the metal heats up—like when a mechanic's hands warm it while they're working."

Willa's eyes widened as she glanced around the hangar, making sure they weren't being watched. "So that's how they're doing it. Quiet, undetectable—poisoned metal. This isn't just sabotage; it's a targeted attack."

Grimble nodded, a steely resolve in his gaze. "Someone's gone to a lot of trouble to make sure these aircraft aren't safe. And whoever they are, they're right here on base."

He glanced over at Fiddler, who was monitoring nearby radio traffic with his Whisper Web. "Fiddler, I need you to keep your ears open. If this is part of a larger plot, there's bound to be more chatter. And we're going to need every scrap of intel we can get."

Fiddler gave a quick nod, adjusting his headphones. "You got it, Major. I'll sift through every transmission until we find our saboteur."

As they slipped back into the shadows, Grimble felt the weight of their mission settle over him. RAF Grantham was a vital stronghold for the Allied forces, and the last thing they needed was a hidden enemy sabotaging their strength from within. Whoever was behind this attack would soon realize that they'd picked the wrong airfield—and the wrong gnome squadron—to mess with.

Section 2: The Investigation Begins

RAF Grantham, Hangar 4, the Following Morning

The next morning dawned cold and foggy over RAF Grantham. Mechanics and crew shuffled between the hangars, their voices low and filled with murmurs of concern. Word had spread quickly that something was amiss; three more mechanics had fallen ill after working on the same aircraft, and rumors of sabotage had begun to ripple across the base.

Major Grimble Pebblewhisker, leader of Squadron 7G, surveyed the hangar from his hiding spot near the rafters, his small, sharp eyes taking in the scene below. The air was tense as humans gathered in small clusters, sharing their theories in hushed tones. But Grimble's focus was on the tall, stern figure who had just arrived—a human officer in a neatly pressed uniform, clipboard in hand and an air of authority that marked him as someone who wasn't there for a routine visit.

"That's Inspector Huxley," Willa whispered from beside Grimble. She'd recognized the officer from one of her recon missions over the nearby bases. "RAF's top investigator. If he's here, then the brass must be getting worried."

"Worried or not, we'll have to work around him," Grimble muttered. "The last thing we need is for the humans to start asking too many questions. Our job is to stay out of sight, get the information we need, and neutralize this threat."

Below, Inspector Huxley had already begun questioning the mechanics, his sharp gaze missing nothing. His questions were direct and to the point, his brow furrowed as he listened to each account of sudden illness and strange symptoms. But he was also skeptical, dismissing the idea of sabotage and suggesting it might be a "temporary issue with supplies" or "a touch of flu." Yet the pattern was undeniable: every mechanic who'd fallen ill had worked on the same aircraft.

Grimble signaled to his team. "Alright, let's get to work. Fiddler, you're on surveillance—keep tabs on Huxley's conversations. Sparks, run another scan on the metal surfaces in the hangar. If our saboteur left any trace, I want to find it."

Fiddler gave a sharp nod and adjusted his Whisper Web headset, his enchanted device tuned to intercept conversations within a 30-foot range. Sparks slipped into the shadows, his small toolbelt clinking softly as he readied his enchanted detection powder.

Willa, meanwhile, kept watch from her vantage point, her keen eyes scanning for any sign that their presence might be noticed. "Huxley's not the only one we need to worry about," she whispered. "The mechanics are getting nervous. It's only a matter of time before one of them starts asking why they keep falling sick."

Grimble nodded. "That's why we need answers quickly—and why we can't afford to make any mistakes."

Huxley's Growing Suspicion

As Grimble's team moved through the hangar, staying out of sight, Huxley continued his investigation, occasionally jotting notes onto his clipboard. But as the morning wore on, he began to notice strange, unexplainable details—tiny boot prints near the aircraft, misplaced tools, and strange markings on the surfaces of some equipment. None of it made sense to him, and he quickly grew frustrated, sensing that something was being kept from him.

Finally, Huxley pulled one of the senior mechanics aside. "Has anyone else been around these aircraft? Anyone unusual?"

The mechanic hesitated, casting a glance over his shoulder. "No, sir. Just us. But… I did notice something strange last night. I could have sworn I saw small figures—maybe animals or birds—

darting around the hangar. Probably just shadows, sir, but…"

Huxley's eyes narrowed. "Shadows, you say?"

The mechanic nodded, looking embarrassed. "I know it sounds odd, sir. Maybe it was just my eyes playing tricks on me, but with all these illnesses, it's hard not to worry."

Huxley made a note, although he didn't comment further. But as he turned back to the aircraft, a strange feeling crept over him. There was something unusual happening at RAF Grantham, and he was determined to uncover it—even if it meant chasing shadows.

The Gnomes' Discovery

Meanwhile, Sparks was busy scanning the aircraft parts, his detection powder glowing faintly as he worked. After a few minutes, he found a spot on the underside of the wing where the powder turned a sickly green—a sign of the same toxic residue they'd discovered the night before.

"Got it, Major," he whispered, gesturing to Grimble. "Same residue as last night. It's faint, but it's there."

Grimble crouched beside him, examining the spot. "It's embedded in the finish. Whoever did this knows exactly what they're doing."

Willa, who had been keeping an eye on Huxley from the rafters, joined them, her expression tense. "This means someone on base has access to specialized materials and knowledge of how to poison them. We're not dealing with just anyone."

Grimble's face hardened. "We're dealing with someone who's familiar with military-grade parts and trained in sabotage. This isn't random; it's targeted."

As they continued their examination, Fiddler suddenly perked up, his Whisper Web headset crackling. He gestured urgently to Grimble. "Major, I'm picking up something odd. Huxley's just received a message over the human frequency. Apparently, he's noticed 'unusual activity' around the hangar. He's calling for a more thorough investigation."

Grimble cursed under his breath. "We're going to need to be even more careful. If Huxley catches wind of our operation, the entire investigation could be jeopardized."

A Growing Collaboration

By early afternoon, Grimble was beginning to realize they wouldn't get far without some collaboration with Huxley. He could feel the investigation stalling, and it was only a matter of time before the human investigators became too aware of their presence.

After a long moment of deliberation, he signaled for his team to regroup. "Listen up, everyone. It's risky, but we're going to make contact with Inspector Huxley. He may be skeptical, but we need his help if we're going to solve this."

The team exchanged glances, each of them understanding the risks. But they trusted Grimble's judgment and knew that working alongside Huxley might be their best chance of uncovering the saboteur.

They waited until Huxley was alone, making sure the mechanics were preoccupied with a debriefing across the airfield. Then, Grimble stepped out of the shadows, clearing his throat to get Huxley's attention.

The inspector whirled around, his eyes widening as he took in the sight of Grimble and his team, each one standing confidently despite their small size.

"What... what is this?" Huxley stammered, his eyes flicking between the gnomes, clearly struggling to process what he was seeing.

Grimble gave a brisk nod, his expression serious. "Inspector Huxley, I'm Major Grimble Pebblewhisker, commanding officer of Squadron 7G. We're part of a specialized intelligence unit, working alongside the RAF to counter enemy threats."

Huxley blinked, taking a step back, still staring in disbelief. "You're... you're gnomes. How is this possible?"

"Impossible or not, we're here," Grimble replied, his voice steady. "And we're here to help. There's a saboteur on this base, one who's found a way to poison aircraft parts. We believe they're receiving coded instructions from outside sources, possibly hidden in routine communications."

Huxley looked at Grimble, then at the rest of the team, his skepticism giving way to curiosity. After a long moment, he nodded, the initial shock fading. "Very well, Major. I'll accept your presence... for now. But I want full transparency on whatever you find."

Grimble nodded in return. "Agreed. But understand this, Inspector—we work in secrecy for a reason. Our role is to handle threats that humans aren't equipped to face, and we need your cooperation to ensure that remains undiscovered."

Huxley's expression softened slightly. "I understand. If there's sabotage at work here, then we'll need every advantage we can get. Let's get to work."

Combining Forces

With a newfound understanding, Grimble and Huxley moved swiftly to combine their resources. The gnomes provided insights into the unusual poison embedded in the aircraft, while Huxley used his authority to secure access to service records, personnel files, and other critical documents.

As the afternoon wore on, the investigation began to pick up speed. The combined team traced the poisoned metal back to a specific batch of parts shipped in from a supply depot in the south—a depot that had recently been flagged for inconsistencies in its records.

Fiddler intercepted another transmission—a coded weather report that, upon closer inspection, contained unusual terminology. Grimble's eyes narrowed as he examined the report.

"This isn't just a weather report," he murmured. "These are instructions, embedded in code.

Whoever our saboteur is, they're receiving orders through the weather updates."

Huxley raised an eyebrow, impressed. "A clever method. Weather reports would pass unnoticed by most, but with the right key, they could contain all kinds of information."

Grimble nodded. "Now we just need to find the person responsible for receiving them. And if we can intercept their next move, we might have a chance to stop them."

Section 3: Working Together

RAF Grantham, Late Afternoon

By late afternoon, Grimble Pebblewhisker and Inspector Huxley had set up a covert command center in a small, unused storage room at the edge of the airfield. It was just big enough for Huxley's paperwork and the gnomes' Whisper Web, but the improvised office crackled with tension and activity. Their investigation had taken on a new urgency—every clue hinted at a vast and sophisticated network, all designed to sabotage the Allies' air capabilities from within.

Huxley leaned over a map of RAF Grantham and the surrounding bases, his brow furrowed. "If these poisoned parts are coming from the depot in the south, then our saboteur has to have connections beyond this base. But the question is, how is he pulling it off without raising suspicion?"

Grimble stroked his chin thoughtfully, his small face etched with concentration. "It's the coded weather reports. They've got instructions embedded in them, and our saboteur must have access to a decryption key." He looked at Fiddler, who was carefully transcribing the intercepted report. "Any progress on decoding that transmission, Fiddler?"

Fiddler glanced up, adjusting his magnified goggles. "Just about, Major. The language is disguised with weather terms, but if you rearrange the words based on coordinates, it gives specific orders." He pointed to a line in the transcription. "Here, for example, 'Windy front passing at dawn' translates to 'incoming parts delivery' at a particular time and location."

Huxley's eyes widened. "A full sabotage schedule hidden in plain sight. They've weaponized routine communication."

Grimble's expression turned grim. "And if that's the case, our saboteur knows more than just how to poison metal. They're getting operational intel directly from the enemy."

Building Trust and Strategy

Over the next few hours, Grimble and Huxley continued to dig through records, transcripts, and even supply chain documents. Huxley was thorough, a by-the-book investigator who left no detail unexamined, while Grimble's experience in intelligence gave him an edge in spotting subtle patterns and connections.

Despite his initial skepticism, Huxley had to admit he was impressed with the gnome unit. He marveled at their tools—especially the Whisper Web, which picked up faint conversations in the hangars with the precision of an advanced human radio. And for their part, the gnomes came to appreciate Huxley's methodical approach and his willingness to think beyond the usual bounds of human investigation.

"You've got a sharp eye, Inspector," Grimble remarked, his voice laced with respect. "If it weren't for your insights, we might have missed the pattern in these reports."

Huxley inclined his head slightly, an unusual warmth in his gaze. "And if it weren't for you and your team, Major, we'd still be dismissing this as a fluke. It's clear that the enemy knows our weaknesses all too well. Which makes me think…"

He trailed off, tapping his chin thoughtfully.

"What is it?" Grimble asked, leaning forward.

"Whoever this saboteur is," Huxley continued, "they're not acting alone. There's a network here, and I suspect it goes higher than a single officer. Perhaps even into command."

Deepening the Investigation

With this new perspective, the combined team decided to split up and gather additional intel. Huxley would interview the mechanics and airfield personnel again, this time using pointed questions to identify anyone who might have received unusual orders or behaved suspiciously. Meanwhile, Grimble and his team would work in the shadows, monitoring the depot's incoming shipments and following any anomalies.

As dusk settled over the base, Huxley began his rounds, asking seemingly casual questions that probed at shifts in behavior and unusual instructions. He noted anyone who hesitated, wrote down each pause and stutter, watching for patterns in their answers.

Meanwhile, Grimble and his team moved quietly through the hangars, examining every shipment label, cross-checking delivery manifests, and searching for evidence of tampering. Sparks, ever the tinkerer, used a miniature enchanted magnifying glass to scan each part's surface for poison residue, his sharp eyes catching even the smallest trace of contaminants.

The investigation was slow, tedious work. But as the hours ticked by, they began to see a pattern emerging—a faint but definite trail that pointed to a single officer with access to both the depot shipments and the encrypted messages.

The Discovery of Lieutenant Bellamy

Fiddler's voice came through the Whisper Web, barely a whisper as he called to Grimble. "Major, I think I've found something. Our suspect might be... Lieutenant Bellamy. He's been the one signing off on these poisoned parts."

Grimble's eyes narrowed. "Are you certain?"

"As certain as we can be without arresting him," Fiddler replied. "But his name keeps popping up on the manifest records for the past few months. He's been working late, intercepting shipments, and ordering specific parts that match those we've found with the toxic finish."

Huxley, who had overheard the exchange, leaned in. "Lieutenant Bellamy. That's a bold move... he's well-respected here. Even the base commander trusts him. But if he's acting on orders from outside..."

Grimble finished the thought. "Then he's been playing everyone, carefully and quietly, feeding the enemy information and sabotaging equipment with no one the wiser."

"Which means," Huxley continued, his voice hard, "he's due for an interrogation."

Planting the Trap

With their target identified, the team devised a plan to confirm Bellamy's guilt and, ideally, lure him into revealing his network. They decided to create a fake coded message using their intercepted weather report technique, scheduling a fake parts shipment to see if Bellamy would tamper with it. It was a gamble, but if Bellamy fell for it, they'd catch him in the act.

Sparks grinned as he finished crafting the fake message, carefully encoding it with the same terminology used in previous reports. "All set, Major. If Bellamy's got any sense, he'll take the bait. And we'll be there waiting for him."

Willa nodded, her eyes gleaming with anticipation. "I'll keep watch near the loading bay. If he shows, I'll signal."

Grimble turned to Huxley. "Inspector, if this works, we'll need to move quickly. There's no telling what Bellamy will do if he realizes he's been exposed."

Huxley nodded firmly. "Understood. I'll be ready."

The Trap is Set

The next night, they put their plan into action. The false weather report had been circulated, carefully timed to match the depot's usual delivery schedule. Huxley and the gnomes hid around the loading bay, each one prepared for the confrontation. Willa positioned herself near the edge of the bay, her sharp eyes trained on the entrance as she waited for Bellamy to appear.

It was nearly midnight when Bellamy arrived, glancing around nervously as he slipped into the shadows. He approached the shipment crate, his face tense as he checked the manifest.

"Now," Grimble whispered, signaling his team.

In a swift motion, the gnomes emerged, surrounding Bellamy as Huxley stepped forward, blocking his escape. Bellamy froze, his face going pale as he realized he'd been caught.

"Lieutenant Bellamy," Huxley said, his voice cold and commanding. "We know what you've been doing. The poisoned parts, the sabotage. Care to explain?"

Bellamy's eyes darted between them, his jaw clenched. For a moment, he looked like he might deny it—but then he exhaled, his shoulders sagging as the truth sank in.

"You don't understand," he said, his voice hoarse. "They threatened my family. If I didn't follow their orders, they said… they said they'd kill them."

Grimble's eyes narrowed. "The Germans?"

Bellamy nodded, his voice barely a whisper. "They reached me through coded messages. Told me if I sabotaged a few aircraft here and there, they'd leave my family alone. I didn't want to, but… they left me no choice."

Confession and Capture

With his confession out, Bellamy sank to the ground, his face etched with guilt. Huxley motioned for the MPs to take him into custody, his expression hard but laced with a trace of pity.

As Bellamy was led away, he issued a final warning, his voice low and filled with dread. "You think this ends with me? There are others… and they're using magic—dark magic. They'll come for you next."

Grimble exchanged a look with Huxley, both of them sensing the gravity of Bellamy's words. If the Germans had begun using dark magic, the threat to RAF Grantham was far from over.

Section 4: The Hidden Threat Inside the Metal

RAF Grantham, Early Morning

The morning after Bellamy's capture was unusually quiet. The fog hung thick over RAF Grantham, and while mechanics worked in silence, the tension was palpable. News of Bellamy's betrayal hadn't yet spread, but Grimble knew it was only a matter of time before the truth came out. For now, however, they had a bigger mystery to solve: how the enemy had managed to poison the aircraft parts so precisely, and just what kind of poison could remain undetected until it was too late.

Grimble and his team gathered in their makeshift command center, the dim light reflecting off maps, files, and intercepted messages spread across the table. Inspector Huxley stood nearby, sipping a mug of tea as he reviewed the night's findings. They were weary but resolute—Bellamy's capture was a significant victory, but it had only opened the door to more questions.

"Alright, team," Grimble began, his tone steady. "We have confirmation that the Germans are embedding poison within the aircraft metal itself. But how? And why this method?"

Sparks adjusted his goggles, his fingers fidgeting with a small enchanted magnifying lens. "It's clever, really. The poison is absorbed into the metal finish—almost invisible. When a mechanic's hands warm it up, the poison reacts to the heat, releasing just enough toxins to make them ill without outright killing them. Keeps the aircraft in circulation but compromises anyone working on it."

Huxley shook his head, his expression one of disbelief. "It's disturbingly efficient. They're weakening our forces, one mechanic at a time. But how are they doing it without raising any suspicion at the depot?"

Willa crossed her arms, her face set in a determined scowl. "That's what we need to find out. If they can poison metal here, they can do it anywhere. We have to cut them off at the source."

Grimble nodded. "Exactly. We've stopped Bellamy, but we need to ensure there aren't other agents supplying these parts to the other bases. Fiddler, any updates on intercepted communications?"

Fiddler looked up from his Whisper Web headset, his eyes gleaming with excitement. "Actually, yes. I picked up a faint signal from the depot—a message embedded in a routine weather update. It was disguised as maintenance instructions but seems to contain a list of coordinates for delivery points. These points all line up with recent illnesses across the region."

Huxley's face darkened as he realized the implications. "So they're not just targeting Grantham. They're building a network of compromised airbases across Britain."

Examining Poison

The team's next step was to understand the poison itself. Sparks, ever the resourceful engineer, had collected samples of the residue left on the aircraft. In their secluded corner of the base, he set up a small alchemical lab with enchanted instruments—gnome-crafted vials and burners designed to test magical and chemical substances. With a careful hand, he began analyzing the sample under his lens.

"Look here," Sparks said, gesturing for Grimble and Huxley to join him. "The substance has magical traces—a signature enchantment, almost like a binding spell. This isn't just a chemical toxin; it's been magically enhanced to bond with the metal."

Grimble's face grew tense. "So we're dealing with a saboteur skilled in both science and magic. It's no wonder the humans never detected it."

Huxley frowned, studying the sample through Sparks' magnifying glass. "You're saying it was enchanted to stay undetected until it made contact with body heat? That kind of work would require expertise… and powerful connections."

"Exactly," Sparks replied. "The kind of connections that would explain why Bellamy mentioned dark magic. Whoever is organizing this sabotage is well beyond the average enemy operative. They have magical allies."

Willa clenched her fists, her eyes flashing with resolve. "Then we have to shut them down, and fast. If dark magic is involved, the stakes are higher than we realized."

A New Lead

As they examined the sample, Fiddler suddenly looked up, his face alight with a new idea. "Major, I think I've cracked part of the message from the weather report. It's encoded, but there's a name hidden within—'The Alchemist.'"

Grimble's eyes narrowed. "The Alchemist?"

Fiddler nodded. "I've heard rumors—an enemy operative, infamous in intelligence circles. Known for blending chemistry and dark magic. If The Alchemist is involved, then we're dealing with a skilled saboteur, possibly the one behind the poison."

Huxley looked troubled. "I've read classified files on The Alchemist. He's been a ghost, rumored to be working with the Nazis, but no one's been able to track him. Until now."

Grimble's face set in determination. "If he's targeting our airbases, then he's no ghost. We have a location, a network, and now a name. Our next mission is clear: we track The Alchemist, stop the flow of poisoned parts, and make sure he never threatens this base—or any other—again."

Tracking The Alchemist

Grimble, Huxley, and the team gathered in a secure area of the hangar to finalize their plans. Their goal was twofold: to locate The Alchemist's primary supply source, and to stop any shipments heading to RAF Grantham and nearby bases.

"We'll have to be quick," Grimble said. "If The Alchemist realizes Bellamy has been compromised, he might move his operation."

Fiddler held up his Whisper Web headset, tuning it to a secure frequency. "I'll monitor all outgoing messages from the depot and intercept anything related to shipments. If The Alchemist is communicating with his operatives, he won't be able to hide from us."

Huxley nodded, drawing his pistol as he adjusted his gear. "I'll join you in the field. I want to see this Alchemist brought down."

Grimble gave him a steady look. "Then let's get to work."

The Raid on the Depot

Under the cover of darkness, the team moved toward the depot. Willa flew ahead in her gnome-sized Spitfire, scanning the ground for guards while Grimble, Huxley, and Sparks crept through the shadows, careful not to alert anyone to their presence.

The depot was guarded, but it was no match for the stealth and skill of Squadron 7G. They slipped inside, moving with the practiced silence of seasoned operatives. In the heart of the depot, they found a storage room filled with metal parts waiting to be shipped to various airbases.

Sparks approached the crates, his enchanted powder at the ready. He sprinkled it over the parts, watching as the powder glowed green, confirming the presence of poison.

"It's everywhere," Sparks whispered, his voice tinged with horror. "Every part in here has been compromised."

Grimble's jaw tightened. "Then The Alchemist has been poisoning entire shipments. If we don't stop him, these parts could sabotage half the RAF."

Suddenly, they heard footsteps. Grimble signaled for silence as a figure emerged from the shadows, his face obscured by a hooded cloak. He moved with a confident, practiced air as he inspected the crates, muttering an incantation that made the air hum with dark energy.

Fiddler's eyes widened as he recognized the insignia on the man's cloak—a serpent intertwined with a vial. "That's him, Major. The Alchemist."

Grimble nodded. "Then let's make sure he doesn't leave this depot."

Confrontation

In a flash, Grimble and his team sprang into action. Sparks threw an enchanted smoke bomb, filling the room with a thick, glittering mist that disoriented The Alchemist. Huxley leveled his pistol, covering the exits as Grimble and Willa circled the enemy operative.

The Alchemist stumbled, coughing as he tried to push the smoke away with a wave of his hand. "Who dares interrupt my work?" he snarled, his voice dripping with venom.

"Consider this your last shipment, Alchemist," Grimble said, his voice cold. "We know about the poison and the sabotage. You're done."

The Alchemist laughed, his voice sharp and mocking. "You think you've won? I'm just a piece in a much larger plan. Cut me down, and others will take my place."

Huxley took a step forward, his gaze hard. "Then we'll deal with them, too."

With a sudden surge of energy, The Alchemist drew a vial from his cloak, hurling it at the ground. The glass shattered, releasing a cloud of dark, hissing smoke that swirled around him, creating a barrier that obscured him from view.

"Don't let him escape!" Grimble shouted, but it was too late. The smoke dissipated, and The Alchemist had vanished, leaving only the echo of his mocking laughter in the empty depot.

Securing the Poisoned Parts

Though The Alchemist had escaped, Squadron 7G and Huxley quickly secured the poisoned parts, ensuring none would leave the depot. Huxley called in reinforcements to confiscate the tainted supplies, and with the threat contained, the base could begin to heal.

As dawn broke over the depot, Grimble gathered his team, his face set with determination. "We stopped this shipment, and that's a victory. But The Alchemist will regroup, and when he does, we'll be ready. Because as long as Squadron 7G stands, we'll keep Britain safe."

Huxley nodded, a newfound respect in his eyes. "You've got my support, Major. And you'll have my help in finding him again. We've put a dent in his plans today, but we'll finish the job."

Grimble extended a small hand, and Huxley shook it with a firm grip. They had taken down one of the enemy's deadliest threats—and they knew this victory was just the beginning.

Section 5: The Coded Weather Reports

RAF Grantham, Intelligence Hangar, Later That Day

After securing the poisoned parts at the depot, Squadron 7G and Inspector Huxley returned to RAF Grantham. Despite their victory, The Alchemist's escape left an ominous feeling in the air. As the team gathered around a map of Britain, Fiddler tuned into the Whisper Web, intercepting any communications that might reveal The Alchemist's next move.

Grimble looked at his team, his face set with grim determination. "We may have halted his operation here, but The Alchemist won't give up. He escaped for a reason—he's likely planning to regroup, maybe even escalate his attacks. We need to find out where he's headed next."

Huxley, standing nearby, studied the map with a serious expression. "If he's using coded messages embedded in weather reports, there may be more to uncover. It's possible he's been using this method for months, sending instructions across his entire network."

Fiddler adjusted his headset, narrowing his eyes as he analyzed the latest intercepted report. "I think I'm starting to see a pattern, Major. The Alchemist isn't just targeting Grantham—he's coordinating attacks across a line of RAF bases along the southeast coast."

Grimble's eyes narrowed as he took in the news. "The southeast coast... If those bases fall, he could open a corridor for enemy aircraft to reach London."

Willa leaned forward, her face filled with concern. "That's a direct threat to Britain's air defenses. If The Alchemist succeeds, he could cripple the RAF's ability to respond to an invasion."

Decoding the Latest Message

Fiddler worked quickly, analyzing the intercepted weather report with practiced precision. He adjusted dials, filtering out noise as he decoded each line of the transmission. Finally, he looked up, his eyes sharp with understanding.

"This message is different from the others," he said, gesturing to the transcription. "It's a set of coordinates, matching known RAF locations. But the report also includes times and dates. It looks like he's scheduling specific sabotage operations at each base, one by one."

Grimble's face darkened. "So he's planning a coordinated assault. If we don't stop him, he'll bring down each base systematically."

Huxley studied the decoded message, nodding slowly. "These times line up with scheduled parts deliveries. He's using the shipments to slip his poisoned parts into the system, sabotaging aircraft before they can be deployed."

Grimble exchanged a glance with his team, the gravity of the situation clear. "This is bigger than we thought. If we're going to stop The Alchemist, we'll have to intercept each of these shipments and warn the other bases."

Coordinating the Defense

With the new intel in hand, Grimble and Huxley quickly coordinated with other RAF commanders, alerting them to the threat of poisoned parts. It was a delicate operation—Huxley couldn't reveal the existence of Squadron 7G, so he framed the warnings as "classified intelligence" from an undisclosed source.

Meanwhile, Grimble dispatched Willa to scout the locations listed in The Alchemist's message. Flying low in her gnome-sized Spitfire, she sped along the southeast coast, gathering intel on each targeted base and verifying the delivery routes.

When she returned that evening, her face was serious. "Major, I saw a few suspicious crates at each base, just like the ones we found at the depot. But they're heavily guarded, and the guards don't look like standard personnel. They're... different. Darker."

Grimble's eyes narrowed. "Dark magic, perhaps? The Alchemist might have left his own forces in place to ensure no one interferes."

Huxley looked thoughtful, rubbing his chin. "If he's got dark magic users embedded at each base, this goes beyond sabotage. It's a coordinated assault."

Formulating a Plan

Grimble and his team gathered around the map, their minds racing as they strategized. They had to act fast, but they couldn't spread themselves too thin. With the help of the Whisper Web, they mapped out a route to intercept The Alchemist's forces at each location.

"We'll need to hit the most critical bases first," Grimble said, tracing a line along the southeast coast. "If we can cut off his forces here, we'll disrupt his entire operation."

Sparks grinned, already reaching for his tools. "Then let's go in prepared. I've got a few enchanted devices that'll disrupt any dark magic they're using. Won't stop them completely, but it'll make things difficult for them."

Fiddler nodded, adjusting the Whisper Web's frequency. "I'll monitor The Alchemist's communications. If he tries to send any more coded orders, we'll intercept them."

Huxley looked at Grimble, his face filled with admiration. "Your team is... impressive, Major. This operation is critical, and I'm honored to work alongside you."

Grimble gave him a small nod. "Then let's get to work, Inspector. We have no time to waste."

The First Base: Interception in Action

Their first stop was RAF Dover, one of the bases marked in The Alchemist's message. The gnomes and Huxley arrived just as a shipment of parts was being unloaded. Grimble signaled for silence as they approached the crates, each one labeled with coded markings matching the intercepted message.

Sparks quickly scanned the crates, applying his enchanted powder. Within moments, a green glow spread across the surface, confirming the presence of poison.

"Confirmed," he whispered. "These parts are definitely compromised."

Huxley turned to Grimble, his jaw set. "If they're expecting reinforcements, we'll need to move quickly. Can we disable these parts?"

Sparks grinned, already pulling out his enchanted tools. "Just leave it to me, Inspector. I'll make sure these won't harm anyone ever again."

Working swiftly, Sparks used a neutralizing spell to disarm the poisoned parts, ensuring they wouldn't affect the mechanics. Meanwhile, Willa kept watch, her eyes trained on the perimeter as Fiddler monitored the Whisper Web.

"Major," Fiddler whispered, his voice tense. "I'm picking up a transmission. The Alchemist's forces are on their way—they must have realized something's wrong."

Grimble's eyes hardened. "Then we're out of time. Prepare for an ambush, team."

The Ambush

Just as they finished neutralizing the poisoned parts, shadows appeared at the edge of the base. A group of dark-cloaked figures emerged, each one bearing a faint, sinister glow. They moved with purpose, their hands raised as they muttered spells that filled the air with a chill.

Grimble signaled his team to spread out, each member taking up a defensive position. Sparks tossed a smoke bomb, creating a thick fog that obscured their movements. Willa took to the skies in her Spitfire, circling above and ready to dive at a moment's notice.

The dark figures paused, momentarily disoriented by the smoke. But The Alchemist's forces were no amateurs—they quickly regrouped, forming a circle as they muttered a spell that cleared the fog, their eyes locking onto the gnomes with chilling intensity.

"Stand your ground, Squadron 7G!" Grimble shouted, drawing his enchanted blaster. "These saboteurs don't know who they're dealing with."

A fierce battle erupted, magic and spells crackling through the air as the gnomes defended the base. Sparks hurled enchanted flares that disrupted the enemy's magic, while Fiddler monitored the enemy's movements, directing his teammates as they fought.

Huxley fired his pistol, covering the gnomes' flank as Grimble and Willa took on the leader of the group—a tall, hooded figure whose eyes glowed with a strange, eerie light. The figure raised his hand, summoning a wave of dark energy that shot toward Grimble.

But Willa swooped in, firing a burst of magical rounds that intercepted the spell, breaking it apart mid-air. "Not on my watch!" she shouted, her voice filled with defiance.

The enemy forces faltered, momentarily thrown off balance. Sensing their chance, Grimble and his team pressed forward, each gnome moving with practiced precision as they dismantled the saboteurs' defenses.

Within moments, the enemy forces broke ranks, retreating into the shadows as they realized they were outmatched. The leader cast one last, vengeful look at Grimble before disappearing into the night, leaving the base secure and The Alchemist's operation in disarray.

A Hard-Earned Victory

As dawn broke over RAF Dover, Grimble and his team regrouped, exhausted but triumphant. The poisoned parts had been neutralized, and The Alchemist's forces had been driven back, though not defeated.

Huxley looked at Grimble, his eyes filled with gratitude. "You and your team just saved this base,

Major. And if The Alchemist is as desperate as he seems, this is far from over."

Grimble nodded, his expression serious. "This was only a skirmish. The Alchemist may be weakened, but he's not finished. He'll regroup, and we'll be ready."

Willa adjusted her goggles, a spark of excitement in her eyes. "Wherever he's hiding, we'll find him. No one threatens Squadron 7G and gets away with it."

The team shared a quiet moment of determination, each one knowing the fight was far from over. They had struck a blow against The Alchemist's forces, but they knew that more challenges lay ahead.

Section 6: The Mole is Revealed

RAF Grantham, Early Morning

Following their narrow victory at RAF Dover, Squadron 7G and Inspector Huxley returned to Grantham under a veil of silence. They had driven back The Alchemist's forces, but his network was still active, and the mysterious operative was still at large. Grimble and his team were certain of one thing: their enemy was working from within, hidden in plain sight at RAF Grantham itself.

The fog of early morning clung to the base as Grimble, Fiddler, Sparks, and Willa gathered around their intelligence map. Inspector Huxley joined them, his face set with determination as he spread out the intercepted weather reports that Fiddler had decoded over the last few days.

"We know The Alchemist's been targeting multiple bases," Huxley began, his voice low. "But all roads seem to lead back here, to Grantham. This base is the central hub, and the coded messages suggest someone here is coordinating with The Alchemist."

Grimble nodded. "We've known there was a mole here for some time, but whoever it is, they're careful. They've hidden their tracks well. The question is… who?"

Fiddler scanned the coded reports one more time, his brow furrowed. "I've cross-referenced every name on the recent duty rosters, matching them with the times these messages were intercepted. Only a few people had access to all the restricted areas we've investigated."

Sparks leaned over the reports, adjusting his magnifying goggles. "And only one of them had authorization to sign off on every single shipment. That's how they've been sneaking in the poisoned parts—using the authorization of someone we'd least suspect."

Grimble's eyes narrowed as he followed Sparks' gaze. They'd finally identified their suspect—a figure who had been at RAF Grantham for years, trusted by the entire base: **Lieutenant George Bellamy**, an officer responsible for logistics and supply coordination.

The Discovery of Lieutenant Bellamy's Role

Grimble's face darkened as he considered the implications. Bellamy had been the one in charge of inspecting incoming shipments, overseeing parts, and reporting inventory numbers. He had the authority, the access, and now they realized, the opportunity to sabotage with precision.

"So, he's been The Alchemist's inside man all along," Willa said, her voice tinged with anger. "That explains why every poisoned part seemed to pass through his hands."

Huxley's expression was equally grim. "Bellamy's been hiding in plain sight, using his position to orchestrate the sabotage. He must have been intercepting The Alchemist's orders in the weather reports and acting as the go-between."

Fiddler's Whisper Web crackled, and he quickly adjusted the signal to pick up a new transmission. "Major, there's something… something strange coming through. It's Bellamy."

The team fell silent, listening closely as the transmission played out over the Whisper Web. Bellamy's voice came through, tense and hurried. "This is Bellamy. Plans have been compromised. Abort the shipment. I repeat, abort. Rendezvous at secondary location."

Grimble's eyes flashed. "He knows we're onto him. He's trying to cover his tracks."

Huxley's jaw tightened. "Then it's time we confront him. If he's aware we're closing in, he'll try to escape—and take everything he knows about The Alchemist with him."

Grimble nodded, signaling his team to prepare. "This is our chance. Let's make sure he doesn't slip away."

Confronting Bellamy

Later that evening, under the cover of darkness, Grimble's team positioned themselves strategically around Bellamy's office. Sparks and Willa took the perimeter, ensuring no one could enter or leave without their knowledge. Grimble and Huxley waited just outside, listening carefully as Bellamy muttered anxiously to himself, seemingly unaware that he was being watched.

"Alright, Inspector," Grimble whispered. "On my mark."

With a signal, they moved in, slipping silently through the door and cornering Bellamy before he could react. He froze, his face going pale as he saw the determined looks on their faces.

"Lieutenant Bellamy," Huxley began, his voice cold and commanding. "We know everything. The poisoned parts, the coded messages, the orders you've been intercepting. It's over."

Bellamy's gaze darted between Huxley and Grimble, his hand inching toward his desk drawer.

But Grimble noticed the movement and gave a warning growl, his tiny hand resting on his blaster.

"I wouldn't," Grimble said, his voice low. "Unless you want this to end poorly for you."

Bellamy let his hand fall, exhaling heavily as he realized he was outmaneuvered. "You don't understand," he whispered, his face etched with a mixture of fear and desperation. "The Alchemist… he gave me no choice. They threatened my family. They told me if I didn't cooperate…"

"Threatened or not, you betrayed your country," Huxley replied, his tone unyielding. "You put countless lives at risk. Why?"

Bellamy hesitated, his gaze dropping to the floor. "Because… I thought if I followed orders, I could protect them. They told me this was the only way."

Grimble crossed his arms, his expression unrelenting. "What else do you know about The Alchemist's plans?"

Bellamy swallowed, looking away. "He's… he's more than just an enemy operative. The Alchemist has dark allies, and he's working on something big. Some kind of… ritual. He said it would change the course of the war. I don't know much, but he plans to use the sabotaged bases to conduct the ritual."

The Dark Ritual and the Rising Threat

Grimble and Huxley exchanged glances, the gravity of Bellamy's confession sinking in. The Alchemist wasn't simply poisoning parts—he was setting the stage for something far more dangerous. A ritual that, if successful, could have catastrophic consequences.

"So that's why he's been targeting our bases," Huxley murmured. "He's using them as points of power. With dark magic, he could amplify the effects of his sabotage, crippling our air defense in one fell swoop."

Bellamy nodded, looking defeated. "He's gathering forces—rogue wizards, creatures of dark magic. I don't know where or when, but… it's happening soon. That's all I know."

Grimble's expression was grim. "Then you'll come with us. You're going to help us track him down and stop this ritual."

Bellamy looked at Grimble, his face etched with fear. "If I help you… they'll kill me."

"Then I suggest you help us stop them before they get the chance," Grimble replied, his voice unyielding. "You owe that much to the people you put in danger."

Huxley stepped forward, signaling for the MPs to take Bellamy into custody. "We'll place you in protective custody, but you're not going anywhere until this is over."

As Bellamy was led away, Grimble turned to his team, his face filled with resolve. "This is it. We have confirmation of The Alchemist's plans, and now we know the scale of the threat. It's time to bring an end to this."

Preparing for the Final Battle

With Bellamy's confession fresh in their minds, Grimble and his team gathered to make preparations. They knew the ritual would take place soon, and they needed to be ready to strike before The Alchemist could complete his plans. Using the information they'd gathered, they mapped out the likely locations of the ritual and coordinated a multi-pronged approach to disrupt it.

Sparks was busy enhancing their gear, reinforcing their planes with protective charms and outfitting each member of Squadron 7G with enchanted amulets to guard against dark magic.

"Each of these amulets is bound to a counter-spell," Sparks explained as he handed them out. "If The Alchemist tries to use magic against us, these should help ward off some of the effects. Just don't push them too hard."

Willa adjusted her goggles, a fierce determination in her eyes. "So, we're taking on a whole army of dark magic users, rogue wizards, and who knows what else? Sounds like a challenge."

Grimble nodded, his voice steady. "This is what we've trained for, and we're ready. The Alchemist thinks he can cast a shadow over Britain, but he hasn't met Squadron 7G."

Huxley, who had been listening quietly, stepped forward, his face filled with respect. "It's been an honor working with you all. This battle isn't just about RAF Grantham—it's about the fate of everyone under our protection. Let's make sure we don't let them down."

Grimble nodded, a quiet resolve settling over him. "Then let's move out. Tonight, we put an end to The Alchemist's plans—and make sure he never threatens this base again."

Section 7: Securing the Base and the Ritual Showdown

RAF Grantham, Midnight

The base was eerily quiet as the midnight hour approached. Squadron 7G and Inspector Huxley had worked tirelessly over the last few hours, finalizing their strategy and preparing their equipment. With Lieutenant Bellamy's information and the decoded messages from Fiddler's Whisper Web, they'd pinpointed the location where The Alchemist planned to conduct his ritual—a secluded airfield just outside RAF Grantham, hidden from human sight by a thick layer of enchanted fog.

As the team gathered for final preparations, Grimble surveyed them with pride. Each member of Squadron 7G was equipped with enchanted amulets, protective charms, and a mix of Sparks' latest inventions: smoke bombs, flare traps, and blasters modified for maximum magical disruption.

Grimble nodded, addressing his team. "The Alchemist is attempting to use dark magic to cripple Britain's air defenses, and we're the only line standing between him and success. He's planning to use this ritual to amplify the effects of his sabotage, but if we disrupt it, we can end his plans once and for all."

Huxley's face was set with determination as he tightened the straps on his gear. "He's underestimated us for too long. Tonight, we end this threat."

Sparks flashed a confident grin, patting the small arsenal strapped to his belt. "And with these beauties, we'll make sure he regrets every move he made against RAF Grantham."

Grimble gave his team a final nod, his voice steady. "Stay sharp. The Alchemist won't go down without a fight, and he's prepared for this moment. Let's be sure we're ready, too."

Approaching the Ritual Site

The team moved through the foggy night in silence, guided by the soft hum of Willa's gnome-sized Spitfire flying above, scouting the area for enemy forces. The closer they got to the ritual site, the thicker the air felt, as if charged with dark energy that pulsed like a heartbeat.

Finally, they reached the edge of the field, where faint lights flickered through the fog. In the center of the airfield stood The Alchemist, surrounded by a circle of cloaked figures chanting in unison. Strange symbols had been carved into the ground, each one pulsating with a sinister glow as dark energy seeped from the ritual site and into the air.

Grimble raised his hand, signaling his team to halt. "There he is, at the center. We'll need to break the circle to stop the ritual. Sparks, deploy the flare traps; Willa, take position for aerial support. Fiddler, keep monitoring for any backup on the Whisper Web."

Each team member moved swiftly to their assigned positions, hearts pounding as they prepared for the confrontation.

The Battle Begins

Just as the team positioned themselves, The Alchemist raised his hands, chanting in a strange, guttural language that sent a shiver through the air. His voice reverberated across the field, growing louder as the symbols etched into the ground began to glow brighter.

Willa's voice crackled over Grimble's comm-stone. "Major, the ritual's gaining power. We have to disrupt it now!"

Grimble gave the signal. "Move in! Sparks, now!"

With a flick of his wrist, Sparks hurled an enchanted flare into the center of the ritual. It burst into a blinding flash of silver light, momentarily halting the chant as The Alchemist and his followers recoiled, shielding their eyes.

"Now, team! Disrupt the circle!" Grimble shouted, charging forward.

Squadron 7G sprang into action, darting between the cloaked figures as they planted enchanted flare traps at key points around the circle. Each flare emitted a brilliant glow, creating a barrier that weakened the ritual's energy. Grimble fired a series of precise blaster shots, shattering the symbols carved into the ground and destabilizing the dark magic.

The Alchemist snarled, his eyes flashing with fury as he realized his ritual was unraveling. He raised a hand, summoning dark shadows that coalesced into spectral hounds, each one snarling as it lunged at the gnomes.

"Sparks, Willa—cover our flanks!" Grimble ordered as the hounds closed in.

Sparks deployed another of his enchanted bombs, releasing a burst of light that repelled the spectral creatures. Willa swooped down in her Spitfire, firing enchanted rounds that tore through the shadows, dispelling them in bursts of smoke.

"Nice try, Alchemist," Willa shouted as she looped back for another pass. "But it'll take more than shadows to stop us!"

A Desperate Counterattack

Seeing his forces falter, The Alchemist uttered a furious incantation, his eyes blazing as dark tendrils of energy shot from his hands, aimed directly at Grimble. But Grimble held his ground, activating his enchanted amulet just as the dark magic struck. The amulet flared to life, absorbing the energy and deflecting it harmlessly to the side.

"You'll have to do better than that," Grimble said, his voice steady. "You're not the only one with a few tricks up your sleeve."

The Alchemist sneered, but his face betrayed a flicker of doubt. His ritual was failing, and he could feel the balance shifting against him.

"Your little squad can't stop what's already in motion!" he snarled, desperation creeping into his voice. "My allies are everywhere, and they'll continue my work even if I fall."

Grimble tightened his grip on his blaster. "Your allies will have to find new work. This is where your plans end."

Breaking the Ritual

With each flare deployed, the energy from The Alchemist's ritual weakened further, its glow flickering as the symbols dimmed. Sparks, seeing an opening, pulled out a small vial filled with enchanted nullifying powder—a tool they'd devised specifically for breaking powerful spells.

"Major, if I get close enough, I can neutralize the ritual for good," he called over the comm-stone.

Grimble gave a firm nod. "Go, Sparks. We'll cover you."

Sparks darted forward, zigzagging through the battlefield as he dodged bursts of dark energy and spectral hounds. He reached the center of the ritual, uncorking the vial and pouring the powder into the ground. The powder shimmered, spreading over the symbols and dimming their glow until they faded completely.

The Alchemist let out a roar of fury as the ritual's power collapsed, the dark energy dissipating into the air like smoke. His followers stumbled, disoriented as their connection to the spell was severed.

"It's done!" Sparks shouted, retreating as the last traces of dark magic evaporated.

The Final Confrontation

Realizing his ritual had been undone, The Alchemist turned his gaze to Grimble, his eyes filled with rage. "You may have stopped this spell," he hissed, "but I'll make sure you don't live to celebrate it."

He raised his hands, summoning a final surge of dark magic aimed directly at Grimble. But before he could unleash the spell, Willa swooped down in her Spitfire, firing a blast that struck his hands, breaking his concentration.

Grimble seized the opportunity, leveling his blaster at The Alchemist. "It's over. Surrender, or face the consequences."

For a moment, The Alchemist hesitated, his expression twisting between fury and fear. But in a final act of defiance, he hurled a vial to the ground, releasing a thick cloud of smoke that enveloped him completely. When the smoke cleared, he was gone, leaving only the faint echo of his mocking laughter.

Securing the Site

With The Alchemist gone and the ritual disrupted, Squadron 7G and Inspector Huxley quickly secured the site. They disarmed the remaining followers, ensuring no trace of dark magic remained. Grimble stood at the center of the field, surveying the remnants of the ritual with a mixture of relief and resolve.

Huxley joined him, his face filled with admiration. "You and your team did it, Major. You've saved more lives than anyone on this base will ever know."

Grimble nodded, his gaze steady. "The Alchemist may have escaped, but his plans are in ruins. We've dismantled his network and neutralized his ritual. He won't be a threat for some time."

Willa joined them, adjusting her goggles with a satisfied grin. "Just another day's work for Squadron 7G, right?"

The team shared a moment of quiet pride, each of them feeling the weight of their victory. They knew The Alchemist was still out there, but they had won a crucial battle, one that had saved countless lives.

Section 8: Epilogue and Reflections

RAF Grantham, Dawn

The first light of dawn crept over RAF Grantham, illuminating the base in a calm, golden glow. Squadron 7G, worn and weary from the night's battle, made their way back to their hidden hangar in silence, each member absorbed in their own thoughts. They had dismantled The Alchemist's ritual and stopped his plan to cripple Britain's defenses, but the enemy's escape left an unspoken tension hanging in the air.

Once back in the safety of their hangar, the gnomes set about tending to their equipment, checking for damage and cleaning up their enchanted tools. Sparks patched up Willa's Spitfire, his hands moving with practiced precision as he tightened bolts and checked the wings for damage. Fiddler tuned the Whisper Web, scanning the frequencies for any remaining trace of The Alchemist's network, though he knew it was unlikely.

Finally, Grimble gathered them around the table, his voice low but filled with pride. "Last night, we faced one of the deadliest threats this base has ever seen. We thwarted The Alchemist's plan and kept the enemy from gaining a foothold in our defenses.

Each of you played a part in this victory, and I couldn't be prouder."

The team exchanged quiet smiles, a sense of accomplishment settling over them. Willa gave Grimble a small, mischievous salute. "We'd follow you anywhere, Major. You lead; we fight."

Grimble nodded, his face softening as he looked around at each of them. "This was a victory, but we know The Alchemist is still out there. He'll likely regroup, and he'll come back stronger. We may not know when or how, but we'll be ready when he does."

A Farewell with Huxley

A knock at the hangar door interrupted their moment of quiet reflection. Inspector Huxley stepped inside, his uniform rumpled but his face filled with gratitude as he looked at the team. "Major Pebblewhisker, Squadron 7G—you saved RAF Grantham and protected countless lives. The men on this base will never know the full extent of your work, but I want you to know that I do, and I thank you."

Grimble gave Huxley a firm nod. "Your support was essential, Inspector. Without your help, we might never have tracked down the saboteur or disrupted The Alchemist's network."

Huxley smiled, a trace of humor in his eyes. "I'll admit, working with a gnome squadron wasn't exactly in the handbook. But you're some of the finest operatives I've ever met. It was an honor to work beside you."

He extended a hand, and Grimble shook it firmly, a bond of mutual respect and gratitude passing between them. "If you ever need us, you know where to find us, Inspector."

Looking to the Future

After Huxley left, the team took a moment to decompress, sharing a small breakfast of tea and biscuits in the hangar. Sparks passed around a tin of chocolate he'd saved for special occasions, and they clinked their teacups together in a quiet toast.

"To victories big and small," Fiddler said, raising his cup with a grin. "And to Squadron 7G, the best team a gnome could ask for."

The others laughed, nodding in agreement. But beneath their laughter was a shared understanding— while they'd won a battle, the war was still ongoing. The Alchemist's escape reminded them that the enemy would continue to evolve, finding new ways to threaten their mission and the people they protected.

Grimble raised his cup, his face filled with quiet determination. "We may be small, but our fight is as large as any. And as long as there's a threat to Britain's safety, Squadron 7G will stand ready to protect it."

As they finished their breakfast, the first calls of the day echoed across the base, and they knew it was time to return to their posts, quietly blending into the background to continue their work. They moved with the confidence of a team that had weathered countless battles and emerged stronger each time, each gnome knowing that they would face whatever lay ahead together.

And as Grimble looked out at the sun rising over RAF Grantham, he felt a renewed sense of purpose. Their work was far from over, but as long as they had each other, he knew there was no darkness they couldn't overcome.

The End.

Booklet 3

The Vanishing Pilot Logs: The Covert Mission of Squadron 7G

Section 1: The Disappearing Logbooks

RAF Grantham, Early Morning, 1943

A thick layer of mist clung to the runway as dawn broke over RAF Grantham, casting the base in a muted, gray light. Mechanics and pilots bustled between hangars, preparing for the day's flights, unaware of the invisible tension building just beneath the surface. The past few weeks had seen an unusual series of mishaps—three pilots involved in critical missions had suffered "accidents" on duty, and their logbooks had mysteriously vanished.

Major Grimble Pebblewhisker, a gnome intelligence officer with more field experience than most humans could imagine, strode purposefully toward the RAF's Intelligence Hangar, his small figure cloaked in shadows. His height barely reached the desk's edge, but his presence was unmistakable.

Squadron 7G—RAF Grantham's secret gnome intelligence team—had been called in to investigate the disturbing incidents, and Grimble was ready to get to work.

"Major Pebblewhisker," came a voice from behind. Grimble turned to see **Captain Ellie Ward**, a tall, imposing human officer with sharp eyes and a no-nonsense air about her. She regarded him with a look of curiosity mixed with skepticism.

"Captain Ward, I presume?" Grimble replied, tipping his cap. "I hear you've had some… unfortunate incidents here lately."

Ward nodded, gesturing for him to follow as she walked briskly down the hangar. "That's putting it lightly, Major. Three top pilots, all involved in high-stakes missions, have suffered accidents under suspicious circumstances. And each time, their logbooks went missing before we could review them."

"Odd," Grimble murmured, his brow furrowing. "Logbooks don't just vanish. Someone's removing them on purpose."

"Precisely," Ward replied, a hint of frustration in her tone. "And what's worse, every incident has happened right after a critical mission briefing. I suspect there's a mole on base, but I need proof—and that's why I requested the assistance of your team."

Grimble glanced around the hangar as they walked, his eyes catching the nervous expressions of nearby personnel. The pilots and crew avoided eye contact, whispering to one another as he passed. It was clear that the base was on edge.

"Tell me about these accidents," Grimble said as they reached Ward's office.

Ward pulled out a file, spreading photographs and reports across her desk. "Flight Officer Talbot, for example—an experienced pilot. His plane malfunctioned mid-flight, and he crashed into the coast. He survived, barely, but he remembers nothing of the crash. His logbook, however, was gone by the time his crew reached the scene."

Grimble's eyes narrowed as he studied the photos. "And this happened after a mission briefing?"

Ward nodded. "Yes. We planned a covert operation over German territory, and Talbot was our lead pilot. We're talking about top-secret information, Major—if there's a mole erasing evidence, they're after highly sensitive intel."

Grimble considered her words, his mind racing with possibilities. He'd encountered similar situations in the past—cases where information was erased, altered, or destroyed to hide a trail. But disappearing logbooks suggested something more sinister.

"All right," Grimble said, his voice calm but firm. "Let's bring in my team. We'll need every detail if we're to catch this mole."

Introducing Squadron 7G

Ward led Grimble to an unused storage room on the edge of the airfield, far from the prying eyes of the RAF personnel. It was here that Squadron 7G had set up their temporary command post. The room was cluttered with maps, tiny communication devices, and tools sized perfectly for gnome hands.

Inside, Grimble's team was already hard at work. **Fiddler Twigglehook**, the team's communications expert, was hunched over the Whisper Web—a web of enchanted wires and receivers that allowed him to intercept RAF transmissions. Beside him, **Willa Fernwhisk**, a skilled recon scout, adjusted her miniature flight goggles as she studied the RAF personnel roster, memorizing names and faces. Finally, **Tinker "Sparks" Bogglebright**, the team's inventive engineer, tinkered with a small device, muttering under his breath as he adjusted a dial.

"Listen up, team," Grimble said as he entered. "Captain Ward here is facing a series of vanishing logbooks, all connected to high-level missions. We suspect a mole—possibly using some kind of sabotage technique to erase evidence. Our task is to track them down and secure any remaining intel before it's compromised."

Fiddler looked up from his Whisper Web, a glint of excitement in his eyes. "Intercepted messages, you say? I can sift through the base's recent communications and look for anomalies. If someone's been tampering with logs, they might've sent coded signals."

Sparks adjusted his goggles, grinning. "And if they're using anything enchanted, I've got just the tools to sniff it out. Give me a few minutes with those logbooks, and I'll find any traces of magic."

Ward glanced at the gnomes, her skepticism fading as she saw their focus and professionalism. "I'll admit, I was doubtful about bringing in a gnome unit. But you've got a sharp team, Major."

Grimble gave a modest nod. "We've been at this a long time, Captain. Let's get to work."

The Investigation Begins

Their first order of business was to inspect the pilots' lockers, starting with those belonging to Flight Officer Talbot and the other two pilots involved in the "accidents." Ward led the way, unlocking the small, metal compartments, each of which still held personal items left behind by the injured pilots.

Sparks began by dusting each surface with an enchanted powder that reacted to any trace of magic. To his surprise, a faint shimmer appeared on the inside of Talbot's locker, a residue that was nearly invisible to the naked eye.

"Major," Sparks whispered, gesturing to the locker. "We've got something here—a residue. Looks like it was left by some kind of enchanted ink or tool."

Ward's eyebrows shot up. "Ink?"

Grimble inspected the shimmer closely, his eyes narrowing. "Invisible ink, perhaps? Some types leave a faint trace, detectable only under specific lighting."

Sparks nodded. "Precisely. And it wouldn't be just any ink. Given how well it's concealed, we're likely dealing with something that's enchanted to vanish after use—possibly activated by light."

Ward's face darkened as she considered the implications. "So, whoever's been taking these logbooks could be erasing evidence using an enchanted ink that self-destructs."

Fiddler's fingers flew over the Whisper Web's dials as he scanned the nearby frequencies. "If they're using enchanted ink, they're probably taking precautions to avoid getting caught. I'll monitor outgoing transmissions, see if there's anything unusual being communicated off-base."

Grimble nodded. "Excellent. Captain, let's continue inspecting the area. The more traces we find, the closer we get to identifying our mole."

A Curious Encounter

As they left the locker room, Ward and Grimble were met by a young officer, his face pale and anxious. He stopped short upon seeing Ward, shifting nervously as if caught off guard.

"Captain Ward," he stammered, glancing between her and Grimble. "I… I was just looking for something I misplaced."

Ward gave him a sharp look. "Is that so, Lieutenant? And what might that be?"

The young officer swallowed, his gaze darting to the ground. "A… a notebook. My notebook. I thought it might be in the lockers, but… perhaps I left it elsewhere."

Grimble watched the officer closely, noting the unease in his stance. The behavior was odd, and it struck Grimble as more than mere nervousness—it was as if the officer knew something he was afraid to reveal.

"You're welcome to check the lockers after we're done," Grimble said, his tone polite but firm. "However, it's odd that you'd need a notebook here in the first place."

The officer mumbled something incoherent before hastily excusing himself, disappearing down the hall.

Ward narrowed her eyes. "I don't trust him. He's usually assigned to logistics, far from the flight roster."

Grimble considered her words. "It's possible he's involved, or at the very least, knows something. We'll keep an eye on him. In the meantime, let's follow this ink lead and see where it takes us."

Testing the Invisible Ink Hypothesis

Back in their temporary command post, Sparks carefully collected a sample of the shimmering residue from Talbot's locker, placing it under an enchanted lens that amplified the faint traces of magic. With a twist of the dial, he adjusted the light to test various wavelengths, observing how the residue reacted.

"Fascinating," Sparks muttered, his eyes alight with excitement. "This ink reacts specifically to certain frequencies—look, it's forming letters!"

The others gathered around, watching as faint words appeared on the paper, their shapes barely visible under the magnified lens. The letters seemed to spell out instructions, references to mission details, all meticulously hidden in invisible ink.

"It's a message," Ward whispered, her eyes widening. "Whoever's behind this was altering logs with invisible notes—notes that would self-destruct if exposed to sunlight."

Grimble nodded, his face set with determination. "Then we know our enemy's method. Now we just have to find the person responsible."

He glanced at his team, his eyes gleaming with resolve. "This is no ordinary espionage case. We're up against a spy skilled in magical concealment. Let's keep our wits about us—this is only the beginning."

Section 2: The Investigation Begins

RAF Grantham, Later That Morning

After the initial discovery of the enchanted invisible ink, Major Grimble Pebblewhisker and Captain Ellie Ward wasted no time diving deeper into the mystery. They knew that every minute counted; the enemy had already caused significant damage, and if they didn't act swiftly, more RAF pilots might suffer "accidents." Grimble had his team set up a secure base of operations in an unused section of the airfield, far from prying eyes.

The room was bustling with activity. Sparks was working over a small makeshift lab table, carefully analyzing the residue sample under different light frequencies, while Willa and Fiddler organized the intercepted transmissions, looking for any unusual messages or patterns.

Ward stood beside Grimble, watching the team work with a mix of respect and fascination. "Your team is impressive, Major. Efficient, too."

Grimble gave a modest nod, his eyes focused on Sparks' work. "We've had plenty of practice, Captain. Gnome intelligence units don't usually make headlines, but we're here for precisely these types of cases. Sabotage, espionage, and... invisible ink." He chuckled softly, though his expression remained serious.

Early Clues and Testing the Ink

Sparks adjusted his enchanted lens, studying the residue on a piece of test parchment. The faint shimmer of letters flickered under the magnifying glass, forming cryptic instructions and dates, all related to recent RAF missions.

"Interesting…" Sparks muttered, his voice barely audible over the hum of machinery. "This isn't just any ink. It's been enchanted with a timed spell, designed to fade after a specific period or when exposed to sunlight. Ingenious way to avoid leaving evidence."

Grimble nodded, considering the implications. "So the spy is careful, skilled in both dark magic and intelligence tactics. This isn't a typical case of sabotage. They're destroying these logbooks to erase any trace of their alterations, covering up mission details and compromising our pilots in the process."

Ward's face darkened. "It sounds like they're erasing evidence that might reveal larger plans. And if they've gone to these lengths to cover their tracks, it means they have access to highly sensitive information."

Fiddler looked up from his Whisper Web, adjusting his headset. "Major, I've been monitoring transmissions around the base, and I've picked up a few odd messages in the past couple of days—frequencies that don't match our usual RAF channels. It's almost as if someone's sending coded messages through short-wave transmissions."

Grimble's eyes gleamed with interest. "Good work, Fiddler. Focus on those channels and see if you can decode any messages. If the spy is using invisible ink, there's a high chance they're also sending instructions or reporting back to someone."

Suspicious Activity in the Officer's Quarters

As the team analyzed the ink and reviewed intercepted communications, Captain Ward received a message from one of the maintenance officers, who reported suspicious behavior in the officer's quarters. Apparently, someone had been seen entering Flight Officer Talbot's quarters late at night—someone whose silhouette didn't match Talbot's.

Grimble's face took on a hard edge. "Someone was accessing Talbot's quarters? Then they're trying to cover their tracks, possibly removing anything we might find useful."

Ward nodded, her tone serious. "If we move quickly, we might catch them off guard. I suggest we inspect the quarters for any other clues, in case the spy missed something."

Grimble turned to Willa. "You're on recon. Let's move quietly and keep a low profile. We don't want to alert anyone to our presence just yet."

With that, the team moved through the base, staying to the shadows as they approached the officers' quarters. It was still early morning, and most personnel were busy with their duties, giving them a window of opportunity to investigate undetected.

Inspecting Talbot's Quarters

Talbot's quarters were sparse but neatly kept a reflection of the disciplined pilot. Grimble scanned the room, his keen eyes taking in every detail. Willa moved to the desk, her fingers skimming the surface, searching for any traces of enchanted ink or other magical residue.

"There's something here," Willa whispered, her voice barely audible. She picked up a folded piece of paper hidden beneath a stack of files. It looked ordinary at first glance, but as she tilted it toward the light, faint words shimmered into view, written in the same invisible ink they had encountered in the locker.

Ward leaned in, reading the barely-visible message. "It's a set of coordinates... and an instruction to 'await confirmation on departure.'"

Grimble's brow furrowed. "Coordinates? And confirmation on departure... It sounds like a coded message. Either it's an extraction point, or it's the location where they plan to move the next set of logbooks."

Sparks took out a portable light scanner, focusing it on the paper to reveal more of the message. "The ink's fading fast. We don't have much time to read it before it self-destructs."

Grimble turned to Ward. "This confirms our suspicions. The spy is targeting key mission details, removing and altering records to confuse us. And it seems they're planning another operation soon."

Ward clenched her jaw. "Then we don't have time to lose. Let's see where these coordinates lead."

A Tense Alliance

Back in their command post, the team examined a map of the nearby area, pinpointing the coordinates revealed in Talbot's quarters. The location turned out to be an old farmhouse, about ten miles outside the base—a seemingly ordinary building, but strategically placed near RAF supply routes.

"This farmhouse could be the staging ground for the spy's operations," Grimble said, studying the map closely. "We need to investigate, but we'll need to be cautious. If the spy suspects we're onto them, they might try to flee or destroy any remaining evidence."

Ward looked thoughtful. "I'll arrange for a few trusted RAF personnel to keep watch on the farmhouse from a distance. But for the actual investigation, I think it's best if your team leads the charge. You gnomes are better at moving undetected."

Grimble gave her a nod of approval. "Agreed. We'll take Willa for recon, and Sparks and Fiddler for support. We'll check for any enchanted items, logbooks, or other evidence that might reveal the spy's identity."

Fiddler glanced up from his Whisper Web, his expression serious. "I'll monitor the farmhouse's communications during the operation. If anyone tries to send a signal, I'll intercept it."

Ward hesitated, then spoke quietly. "I'll join you on this mission, Major. I know the terrain well, and it might help to have a human along in case we run into trouble."

Grimble considered her offer, then gave a small nod. "Very well, Captain. But stay close. We move fast and quietly. The last thing we need is for the spy to catch wind of our presence."

Setting Out for the Farmhouse

As dusk fell, Grimble and his team set out toward the farmhouse, sticking to the cover of trees and keeping low to avoid detection. The farmhouse loomed ahead, a dark silhouette against the fading light. It looked abandoned, but Grimble knew better than to trust appearances.

Willa took point, scouting ahead and signaling the all-clear once they reached the building's perimeter. Sparks and Fiddler moved in behind her, while Grimble and Ward followed, staying close as they approached the farmhouse.

Fiddler adjusted his Whisper Web, tuning it to the frequencies used in the previous transmissions. "I'm picking up something," he whispered, his voice barely audible. "It's faint, but there's definitely a signal coming from inside the building."

Grimble's eyes narrowed. "Then we have our target. Move in slowly and watch for any traps or alarms."

Inside the Farmhouse

The team crept into the farmhouse, finding it dark and filled with a thick layer of dust. But amidst the clutter, Grimble noticed a table set up with maps, documents, and a small, flickering lamp. Whoever was using this farmhouse had been here recently, likely planning their next move.

Ward moved to the table, her eyes scanning the documents spread across its surface. "This looks like a list of flight schedules and mission details. They're tracking RAF movements. If this fell into enemy hands…"

Grimble held up a finger, silencing her. He pointed to a faint shimmer on one of the documents—another message written in invisible ink, but this one was still fresh.

Sparks leaned forward, using his light scanner to reveal the message. As the letters took shape, the team read the words aloud, barely believing what they saw: **"Next target: Operation Silver Hawk. Ensure all logbooks are collected. Await further orders."**

Ward's eyes widened. "Operation Silver Hawk… That's classified. If they're targeting that mission, then the entire operation could be at risk."

Grimble's expression hardened. "Then we're out of time. We need to secure these documents, and we need to find this spy before they compromise the operation."

A Sudden Disturbance

Just as they gathered the documents, a noise echoed from the farmhouse entrance—a faint creak, followed by hurried footsteps. Grimble signaled for silence, gesturing for his team to take cover. The farmhouse door opened, and a figure entered, silhouetted against the dim light. Grimble's heart quickened as he recognized the man: **Lieutenant Victor Hale**, a logistics officer at RAF Grantham.

Hale moved quickly, heading straight for the table. He froze when he saw the documents scattered, his face contorting with fury and fear. He knew someone had discovered his operation.

Grimble and Ward emerged from the shadows, blocking the exits. "Lieutenant Hale," Grimble said, his voice cold. "Going somewhere?"

Hale's eyes darted between them, panic flashing across his face. "I… I don't know what you're talking about," he stammered, trying to keep his composure.

"Save it," Ward snapped, her tone icy. "We know you've been altering logbooks and sending enemy intel. You've endangered lives and betrayed your fellow officers."

Hale's expression hardened, his eyes filled with a desperate resolve. "You don't understand… They forced my hand. I had no choice."

Grimble's gaze was unyielding. "Perhaps not. But now, you're going to help us bring this operation to an end."

Section 3: Following the Ink Trail

Inside the Farmhouse, RAF Grantham's Perimeter

Lieutenant Victor Hale stood frozen, his back to the farmhouse wall, his eyes darting around as if looking for an escape. Major Grimble Pebblewhisker, Captain Ellie Ward, and the members of Squadron 7G kept their eyes trained on him, ready to move at the slightest hint of resistance.

"Lieutenant Hale," Ward began, her voice steady but sharp. "You're caught. We've got enough evidence here to show you've been erasing logs and feeding intel to the enemy. You may as well tell us everything you know."

Hale's gaze shifted to the floor, his jaw set tightly. He hesitated, clearly torn between confessing and attempting to stay loyal to his handlers. After a tense moment, he spoke, his voice barely above a whisper.

"You don't understand," he said, his tone pleading. "They made me do it. They threatened my family. I was only supposed to send them small bits of information, minor details that wouldn't affect the war effort. But then they demanded more. The logbooks… the missions… they wanted everything."

Grimble crossed his arms, his small face set in a steely glare. "And so you just handed over critical RAF intelligence? Lives have been put at risk, Hale. Pilots have been injured, their records erased. Was protecting yourself worth that?"

Hale's shoulders slumped, his face filled with guilt. "I thought I could manage it, stay ahead of them. But they've got agents everywhere. If I didn't do what they said, they would've… I had no choice."

Ward took a step closer, her expression cold. "There's always a choice, Lieutenant. And now you'll help us fix the mess you've made."

Hale's Confession

Reluctantly, Hale began to divulge details about his operation. He explained that he'd been recruited by an enemy contact who went by the codename **"The Ghost"**—a shadowy figure with connections throughout the Allied forces. The Ghost had supplied him with enchanted invisible ink, along with instructions to erase key details from pilot logbooks using spells that made the ink disappear under sunlight. Hale's task was simple: to feed The Ghost critical information while leaving no trace behind.

"It was brilliant, really," Hale admitted, almost bitterly. "The ink would only reveal itself under specific wavelengths, ones the RAF doesn't use. I was able to alter flight records, mission reports, anything that could give the enemy an advantage."

Sparks leaned forward, his eyes gleaming with intrigue. "But how did you avoid leaving any magical residue? We found traces of enchantment, but it was faint—almost undetectable."

Hale shook his head. "The ink is self-destructive. It leaves only a faint shimmer after use, but that fades within hours. Unless you know what to look for, you'd never find it."

Grimble exchanged a glance with Ward, their expressions tense. The level of sophistication in the enemy's methods was alarming, suggesting that this wasn't the work of an ordinary saboteur.

"We need to know everything about this Ghost," Grimble said, his voice low. "Where does he operate? How does he communicate?"

Hale hesitated, glancing around nervously. "I don't know where he is, exactly. But he communicates through coded messages embedded in weather reports. Each message carries hidden instructions, and they're often set to self-destruct within days."

Fiddler's eyes widened. "Weather reports? That's how he's been sending messages?"

Hale nodded. "Yes. The Ghost sends instructions in seemingly ordinary reports. It's... it's how I knew which logbooks to alter and what details to erase."

Tracking Down the Ghost's Network

With Hale's confession, Grimble and Ward had a new lead. If The Ghost was using weather reports to coordinate with his network, Fiddler could monitor those reports, searching for unusual patterns or frequencies. The team worked quickly, setting up a monitoring station in the farmhouse to track incoming transmissions.

As Fiddler adjusted his Whisper Web to intercept the specific frequency Hale described, Sparks and Willa examined the remaining documents on the farmhouse table, looking for additional clues. After several tense minutes, Fiddler's eyes lit up.

"Major, I've got something," he whispered, his voice filled with excitement. "There's a message hidden in the latest weather report. It references a 'location change' and instructs all contacts to meet at a specified site for 'final orders.'"

Grimble leaned over, studying the decoded message. "A meeting location? Then the enemy is planning a rendezvous."

Ward's face hardened. "If they're meeting in person, this could be our chance to capture The Ghost—and dismantle this operation for good."

Hale, realizing the gravity of what he'd revealed, looked up at Grimble, his face pale. "You're not planning to go after him, are you? The Ghost is dangerous. He has people everywhere."

Grimble gave him a small, grim smile. "Lieutenant, we're not in the business of letting enemies walk free. If The Ghost is within reach, then we're going after him."

Setting Up the Stakeout

After confirming the details of the hidden message, Grimble and Ward put together a plan to intercept The Ghost at the designated meeting location. According to the weather report, the meeting would take place at an abandoned airfield on the coast—a remote site perfect for secret rendezvous.

Under the cover of night, Grimble's team and a select group of RAF personnel moved out, setting up a secure perimeter around the airfield. Willa flew ahead in her tiny Spitfire, scouting the area from above, while Sparks planted enchanted flare traps around the perimeter to alert the team if anyone attempted to escape.

"We're all set, Major," Sparks reported, adjusting his toolbelt with a determined grin. "The moment anyone tries to leave, those flares will light up the sky."

Grimble gave a firm nod. "Good work. Everyone, stay alert. The Ghost is cunning, and he won't come alone. Be prepared for anything."

As dawn broke over the abandoned airfield, Grimble's team lay in wait, each member ready to spring into action at the first sign of movement.

The Ghost Appears

An hour passed before they saw movement near the airfield. A dark car pulled up, and three figures emerged—one of whom wore a cloak and moved with a slow, deliberate air. Even from a distance, Grimble could sense the aura of authority that surrounded the cloaked figure. It had to be The Ghost.

Ward, watching through binoculars, whispered, "That's him. He matches the description perfectly."

Grimble's voice was a low murmur. "Alright, team. Move in slowly. We don't want him slipping away."

The team crept forward, using the shadows of abandoned buildings for cover. As they approached, they could hear The Ghost speaking in low tones to his companions, issuing orders in a language they couldn't understand.

Grimble signaled for the final approach, his team fanning out to block all exits. They were within striking distance when The Ghost's head jerked up, his eyes narrowing as if sensing their presence.

"Now!" Grimble shouted.

In a blur of motion, the team leapt into action. Sparks activated the flare traps, illuminating the area with a blinding light, while Fiddler jammed any outgoing radio signals to prevent The Ghost from calling for backup.

The Ghost spun around, his face twisted with fury as he realized he was surrounded. But instead of surrendering, he raised his hand, muttering an incantation that sent a wave of dark energy rippling outward.

Grimble staggered, his vision blurring as the spell hit, but he forced himself to stay steady, focusing on the Ghost's figure through the haze. "Don't let him escape! We need him alive!"

The Final Confrontation

The Ghost fought fiercely, his hands glowing with dark magic as he cast spell after spell. Sparks countered with a blast from his enchanted blaster, sending sparks flying as the two forces collided.

Willa swooped down from above, firing enchanted rounds that shattered the protective barrier The Ghost had raised. Grimble charged forward, his blaster drawn as he fired at the ground near The Ghost's feet, creating a cloud of dust that obscured his vision.

For a moment, it seemed as if The Ghost might break free. But Ward moved in, blocking his escape route and pinning him against the wall of the abandoned hangar.

"It's over," she said, her voice cold and unyielding. "You're not going anywhere."

The Ghost looked between Ward and Grimble, his expression one of pure defiance. "You may have stopped me here," he hissed, "but there are others. You've only delayed the inevitable."

Grimble leveled his gaze at him. "That may be true. But as long as there are people like us, your kind will never win."

Extracting Information

With The Ghost subdued, Grimble's team searched his belongings, uncovering coded documents, enchanted vials of invisible ink, and a small book filled with names and coordinates. It was a veritable treasure trove of intelligence—a roadmap to the enemy's entire network.

Ward's eyes gleamed as she examined the documents. "This is it. With this information, we can dismantle the entire spy ring."

The Ghost remained silent, his face twisted with rage as he watched them confiscate his belongings. Grimble leaned in, his voice quiet but firm. "You underestimated us, Ghost. And now, your operation is over."

The Ghost sneered, refusing to speak further. But Grimble knew they had won. With the information they'd gathered, they could secure RAF Grantham and bring the enemy's sabotage efforts to a halt.

Section 4: The Aftermath and Wrapping Up the Mission

RAF Grantham, Intelligence Hangar

With The Ghost securely in custody and the critical documents seized, Grimble's team returned to RAF Grantham to assess and catalog the information they'd captured. The Ghost remained under guard, silent and simmering with resentment, while Ward and Grimble pored over the coded names, frequencies, and instructions hidden within his small notebook.

The notebook, though compact, was a goldmine. Each page revealed aliases, communication channels, and a network of contacts operating across the British Isles. The notebook also contained specific instructions on how to use the enchanted invisible ink, further confirming that The Ghost was coordinating a spy ring dedicated to sabotaging the RAF.

As Grimble and Ward studied the entries, Sparks and Willa sifted through the enchanted vials of ink, analyzing their properties under a specialized gnome lens. Fiddler, meanwhile, monitored communications, alert to any retaliatory moves the spy ring might attempt.

Captain Ward glanced at Grimble, a look of grim satisfaction on her face. "With this information, we'll be able to shut down a major part of the enemy's network. We'll expose their agents and secure our bases. You and your team have saved more lives than you'll ever know, Major."

Grimble gave her a modest nod, though his eyes betrayed a quiet pride. "It's what we're here for, Captain. But the fight's not over yet. With spies this entrenched, they're bound to have other agents. We need to stay vigilant."

Analyzing the Documents

Over the next few days, Grimble's team worked tirelessly to decode every piece of information. Sparks developed a special light frequency scanner to reveal any hidden ink messages on the documents, ensuring nothing was overlooked. Each piece of intel brought them closer to identifying potential spies within the Allied ranks.

As they reviewed The Ghost's contacts, Fiddler intercepted a final transmission, sent to a mysterious contact in Switzerland. The message was brief but ominous: **"The Ghost has fallen. Proceed with caution. Await further instructions."**

Grimble exchanged a glance with Ward, both recognizing the implications. The Ghost's handlers were regrouping and likely preparing for their next move. This meant the battle wasn't truly over.

"They know he's been compromised," Grimble said, his voice edged with concern. "And they'll adapt their strategy. But we'll be ready."

Ward nodded. "We'll tighten our security and put everyone on high alert. Thanks to your team, we've gained an advantage, one we won't squander."

A Private Word with The Ghost

Before The Ghost was transferred to an Allied interrogation facility, Grimble and Ward requested one final meeting with him. The Ghost sat in a secure room, his hands bound, his eyes cold and calculating.

Grimble approached him, his gaze unyielding. "You failed, Ghost. Your network is in shambles, and your plans have been exposed. You underestimated us."

The Ghost sneered, his voice dripping with contempt. "You may have won this round, Major Pebblewhisker, but the war is far from over. There are others like me, more skilled, more ruthless. You'll never stop us all."

Grimble remained calm, unmoved by the threat. "Perhaps. But as long as we stand against you, you'll never succeed."

Ward took a step forward, her voice as steady as Grimble's. "If you think we're going to sit idly by, you're mistaken. Every agent you've placed will be found and brought to justice."

The Ghost held her gaze, his defiance unbroken. "We shall see, Captain Ward. We shall see."

With that, he was escorted out, leaving Grimble and Ward alone to consider his words.

A Quiet Victory

Back at their headquarters, Grimble's team gathered for a well-earned break, sharing a simple meal of tea and biscuits as they recounted the operation. Sparks passed around a tin of chocolates he'd saved for such occasions, and the team shared a toast to their success.

"To Squadron 7G," Fiddler said, raising his teacup with a grin. "And to the best intelligence unit the RAF has never heard of."

The others chuckled, their laughter mingling with the hum of the base. For a brief moment, the tension lifted, replaced by a warm sense of camaraderie and satisfaction. They had faced down a deadly threat, exposed an enemy network, and protected RAF Grantham from harm.

Grimble raised his teacup, his voice steady and filled with quiet pride. "To the team, and to all we protect. As long as we're together, there's no darkness we can't face."

Epilogue: Looking to the Future

The next day, as Squadron 7G prepared to resume their duties, Captain Ward approached Grimble, her expression thoughtful. "We've taken down one part of the enemy's operation, Major, but I doubt they'll stop here. The Ghost was only one piece in a much larger game."

Grimble nodded, his eyes reflecting a mixture of determination and resolve. "We'll be ready, Captain. The enemy may evolve, but so will we. As long as Squadron 7G stands, we'll be a shield against any threat they send our way."

Ward extended her hand, and Grimble shook it with a firm grip. "Thank you, Major. I didn't think I'd see the day when gnomes would be our greatest allies, but you and your team have more than proven your worth."

With that, Ward turned to leave, casting one last look at Grimble and his team. They had faced a formidable enemy together, and she knew that as long as Squadron 7G was around, RAF Grantham would remain protected.

As the sun rose over RAF Grantham, Grimble watched his team with pride. They were small, yes, but their courage and skill made them giants among their comrades. And as they returned to their duties, Grimble knew that whatever challenges lay ahead, Squadron 7G would be ready to face them head-on.

Extended Epilogue: The Shadows Ahead

RAF Grantham, Two Weeks Later

The airfield was alive with activity. Fresh squadrons trained in the skies above, the mechanics tinkered with engines on the ground, and a certain buzz of energy hummed through the base. The successful dismantling of The Ghost's network had sent ripples of relief across RAF Grantham; without ever knowing it, countless lives had been safeguarded. But while most of the personnel could relax, Squadron 7G remained vigilant, knowing their work was far from over.

Inside a hidden corner of the intelligence hangar, Major Grimble Pebblewhisker and his team gathered for a briefing. The past two weeks had been quiet, but reports from neighboring bases indicated signs of unusual activity. It was the kind of calm that Grimble, with his years of experience, knew to distrust.

Fiddler sat at his station, his Whisper Web buzzing faintly as he intercepted faint transmissions from across the region. Sparks worked quietly over his workbench, fiddling with a new invention—a kind of "disruptor light," designed to reveal invisible ink at a safe distance. Willa was nearby, polishing her gnome-sized Spitfire, her eyes sharp with determination.

Grimble looked at his team, his expression one of pride tempered with caution. "The Ghost may be gone, but his network wasn't a one-man operation. We've received intel about unusual troop movements along the coast, coded messages intercepted from allied channels. We'll keep a close watch—if they're gearing up for another attempt, we'll be ready."

Sparks nodded, strapping a freshly enchanted lens to his toolbelt. "If they're using more of that invisible ink, this time we'll spot it a mile away."

A New Arrival

As the team prepared for the possibility of future missions, Captain Ellie Ward appeared at the entrance to their hangar. She carried a box of files, each stamped with the "Top Secret" insignia and marked with codes they hadn't seen before.

"Major Grimble," she greeted him, setting the files down with a wry smile. "HQ's sent over everything they've gathered on The Ghost's associates. They've managed to decrypt a few additional names and locations, and I thought Squadron 7G might like a first look."

Grimble's eyes gleamed with interest as he opened the box, scanning the first file. Each page was a glimpse into the hidden lives of enemy agents, spies who had operated undetected for years, slipping through borders and disguising their actions with remarkable skill. Ward watched him work, her expression thoughtful.

"You know," she said after a moment, "it wasn't long ago that I'd have thought it… unlikely for gnomes to be leading such high-stakes operations. I was skeptical when I first met you, Major."

Grimble looked up, his eyes glinting with amusement. "A little skepticism is healthy, Captain. We're a bit unconventional, I'll grant you that."

Ward's gaze softened. "Unconventional or not, you've set a standard. There are few intelligence teams I'd trust as much as Squadron 7G."

Foreshadowing Future Missions

As Ward departed, Grimble closed the last of the files, setting his sights on the horizon. The Ghost's threat might have been neutralized, but Squadron 7G knew that enemy agents lurked in the shadows, plotting, watching, waiting for their next opportunity.

Grimble gathered his team, giving each member a resolute nod. "We've won a victory, but we can't grow complacent. Our work's not done until every last threat to the RAF is eliminated. From here on out, we operate at full vigilance. No suspicious signal, no report, no detail escapes our notice. Understood?"

The team gave a chorus of affirmations, each member's face set with quiet resolve. They were more than just intelligence operatives; they were protectors, guardians of RAF Grantham and all it stood for.

As dawn broke over the airfield, Squadron 7G returned to their stations, each of them ready to face whatever shadows lay ahead. And in the heart of their hidden hangar, Grimble smiled, knowing that as long as they stood together, there was no darkness they couldn't conquer.

The End.

Booklet 4

The False Orders: The Secret Mission of Squadron 7G

Section 1: The Suspicious Orders

RAF Grantham, Late Night, 1943

It was past midnight at RAF Grantham, and most of the base was quiet, save for the faint sounds of distant engines and the occasional murmur of radio static. Squadron 7G, the RAF's hidden gnome intelligence unit, was supposed to be off duty. But Major Grimble Pebblewhisker, leader of the team, felt a familiar tug of unease pulling him from his bed in their hidden quarters.

Grimble slipped through the shadows of the hangar, his sharp eyes scanning for anything unusual. As he made his way toward the briefing room, he heard faint voices and stopped, listening carefully. The voices were low and urgent—two RAF officers discussing orders for a new mission, one that was set to launch at dawn.

Grimble's curiosity deepened. He hadn't heard anything about a new mission, and it was unusual for orders to come through with such short notice. The voices faded, and Grimble quickly hid as the two officers left the room, heading in opposite directions.

The moment the coast was clear, Grimble slipped into the briefing room, making his way to the map table where the mission papers lay scattered. His eyes scanned the top sheet—a set of coordinates deep inside German-occupied territory, along with flight paths and mission objectives.

A chill ran down Grimble's spine. The mission was too risky, even for an experienced squadron. Something about these orders felt wrong.

Calling in the Team

Back at the Squadron 7G hangar, Grimble assembled his team. Willa Fernwhisk, Fiddler Twigglehook, and Tinker "Sparks" Bogglebright gathered around, each of them looking a mix of groggy and intrigued as they listened to Grimble's report.

"Something's off," Grimble explained, spreading the orders across the table. "These papers instruct an entire squadron to fly deep into enemy territory. They're supposed to take out a weapons facility, but there's no intel on the base defenses, no cover plans for retrieval. Just coordinates and an all-out strike."

Willa narrowed her eyes, her keen instincts kicking in. "That's practically a death sentence. Even with full support, they'd be flying straight into the heart of enemy territory. Who authorized this?"

Grimble shook his head. "That's what we're going to find out. Official orders should come through Command, but there's no record of them anywhere on the Whisper Web or the RAF's intel channels."

Fiddler adjusted his headset, tuning it to pick up any unusual transmissions. "I'll monitor the base frequencies. If there's any rogue transmission, I'll catch it. But if these orders are forged, someone went to great lengths to make them look official."

Sparks looked over the documents, running his finger along the ink. "Give me a few minutes with these, Major. If these papers are fakes, I might be able to spot clues in the material—anything that would give away a forgery."

Grimble nodded. "Good thinking, Sparks. And Willa, I want you to keep watch on the pilots scheduled for this mission. If anyone gets wind of our investigation, they might try to launch the planes before we can stop them."

As the team dispersed to their tasks, Grimble felt the weight of the mission settle over him. Someone had issued these false orders, putting RAF pilots in danger. And until they uncovered the source, they couldn't be sure who to trust.

Examining the Orders

Sparks sat down at his workbench, carefully inspecting the orders under an enchanted lens. He examined every detail—the paper texture, the ink, even the faint imprint of the typewriter keys. After a few minutes, he noticed something unusual: a faint watermark that didn't match the official RAF stationery.

"Major," Sparks said, his voice filled with urgency, "these papers are forgeries. The watermark's all wrong. Official orders come with the RAF crest, but these papers are stamped with a civilian mark—something a supply officer might overlook."

Grimble's expression hardened. "Then whoever forged these orders knows the RAF protocols well. They went to great lengths to make these look authentic but left small details that most wouldn't notice."

Fiddler's voice crackled over the Whisper Web as he tuned into an unusual transmission. "Major, I just intercepted a faint signal—a code sequence being sent to a nearby airfield. It's encrypted, but the timing's suspicious. It could be connected to these orders."

Grimble leaned over Fiddler's station, his mind racing. "Decrypt it if you can. And be ready for anything—this could be a trap."

Following the Signal

Fiddler worked quickly, decoding the transmission. As the words came into focus, his face paled. "It's an update… a set of instructions sent from someone on base to a contact at another location. It reads, 'Mission orders successfully issued. Expect significant losses—air support will be limited.'"

Grimble felt a surge of anger. The forged orders were no accident; they were part of a deliberate plot to weaken the Allied forces. "This isn't sabotage—it's treason. Whoever sent these orders wants our forces to fail."

He turned to his team, his voice calm but urgent. "We're dealing with a double agent. They've been embedded here, using forged orders to send our pilots on suicide missions. And if we don't act fast, this squadron will be the next casualty."

Willa's expression darkened. "Any idea who's behind it?"

Grimble's eyes narrowed. "Not yet. But we'll find them. Fiddler, keep monitoring the base for any unusual activity. Sparks, check the equipment for tampering. And Willa, get eyes on the pilots—if anything looks suspicious, I want to know."

As the team sprang into action, Grimble knew they were racing against the clock. The double agent had planned this operation meticulously, and they'd stop at nothing to see it through. But Squadron 7G was ready—and they'd do whatever it took to protect their allies.

Section 2: Narrowing Down Suspects

RAF Grantham, Early Morning

The sun was just beginning to rise over RAF Grantham as Squadron 7G worked from their hidden intelligence hangar, each team member focused on unraveling the mystery behind the forged orders. Major Grimble Pebblewhisker paced the room, going over every detail in his mind. The squadron scheduled to fly the "mission" was set to leave in less than two hours, and they still didn't have a name for the traitor who'd crafted the suicide mission.

Fiddler sat hunched over the Whisper Web, his headset crackling as he sifted through recent transmissions, searching for anything out of the ordinary. Sparks was running tests on the equipment, checking for signs of tampering or sabotage, while Willa kept tabs on the pilots preparing for takeoff.

"Fiddler," Grimble called over, "anything unusual in those transmissions?"

Fiddler adjusted the dials, concentrating on a series of faint signals. "I'm picking up a few low-frequency pings, all coming from the same location on the other side of the airfield. It's faint, but the timing lines up with the message we intercepted last night. Whoever sent those orders may be hiding nearby."

Grimble's eyes narrowed. "Then we've got our starting point. Let's track it down and see if we can find our mole."

Checking the Airfield

The team split up, each taking a different approach to cover ground quickly. Grimble and Willa made their way across the airfield, staying in the shadows as they approached the location Fiddler had flagged. The building in question was an old storage shed, rarely used and positioned far enough from the main hangars to go unnoticed.

Willa adjusted her goggles, scanning the perimeter for signs of movement. "Looks deserted, but we should assume someone's watching. I'll take the back entrance."

Grimble nodded. "I'll head in from the side. Stay alert—we're likely dealing with someone well-trained."

They moved in synchrony, slipping through the shadows until they reached the shed. Grimble pressed his ear to the door, listening. Inside, he could make out faint murmurs, the sound of papers rustling, and a low hum that suggested someone was using radio equipment.

He signaled for Willa to move in. She opened the back door quietly, catching a glimpse of the interior—a small room cluttered with papers, maps, and a portable radio set. At the center of it all was a man, hunched over a set of documents, completely absorbed in his work.

Grimble recognized him immediately: **Lieutenant Martin Fletcher**, a logistics officer who was typically quiet, kept to himself, and never stood out. The perfect cover for a mole.

Confronting the Suspect

Grimble slipped into the room, signaling Willa to cover the exit. Fletcher looked up in surprise, his eyes widening as he saw Grimble and Willa blocking his escape.

"Lieutenant Fletcher," Grimble said, his tone calm but firm. "Mind explaining what you're doing here?"

Fletcher's eyes darted around, calculating his options. "I was… I was just going over some supply records. Routine checks, nothing unusual."

Willa crossed her arms, her gaze sharp. "In a forgotten storage shed with a portable radio set? Don't insult us, Lieutenant. We know about the forged orders."

Fletcher's face paled, but he quickly composed himself. "Forged orders? I have no idea what you're talking about."

Grimble took a step closer, his eyes locked onto Fletcher's. "We found your transmission signal, Lieutenant. You issued orders for a mission that would send our pilots straight into enemy territory. That's treason. Now, you can either help us stop this mission, or face the consequences."

Fletcher hesitated, his expression shifting between fear and defiance. "You don't understand. This isn't… it's not what it looks like. I'm doing what I have to."

Willa's eyes narrowed. "You're working with the enemy, aren't you?"

Fletcher looked down, his shoulders slumping in defeat. "Yes, but it's not by choice. They found leverage on me—family, people I couldn't protect. They told me if I cooperated, no one would get hurt."

Grimble's face softened, but his voice remained steady. "So you forged orders, risking the lives of your fellow soldiers? You could have come to us, Fletcher. We could have helped."

Fletcher shook his head. "No one can help. The people I'm dealing with… they're everywhere. If I didn't comply, they would have killed me and my family."

Uncovering the Plan

Fletcher slumped down onto a nearby crate, rubbing his forehead as if the weight of his secret had finally broken him. "The orders were designed to cause chaos. They wanted me to send squadrons into impossible situations, to weaken our defenses. I didn't want to do it, but they left me no choice."

Grimble exchanged a look with Willa, a grim understanding passing between them. "Who's behind this, Fletcher? Who's giving you these orders?"

Fletcher hesitated, his gaze flickering with fear. "A contact known only as 'The Falcon.' He works through intermediaries, sending coded messages that only I can decrypt. The orders… they're usually embedded in supply reports, so no one else notices."

Grimble's expression darkened. "The Falcon. We've heard that name before—an enemy agent, rumored to be coordinating sabotage efforts from within the British ranks."

Willa's eyes sharpened. "Then he's likely got more contacts on base. If we can intercept his next message, we can track down his network."

Laying a Trap

With Fletcher's reluctant cooperation, Grimble and his team devised a plan. They would intercept the next set of forged orders, plant a decoy mission, and trace any contacts who responded to The Falcon's instructions.

Fiddler set up his Whisper Web to monitor the supply channels, while Sparks rigged a light-sensitive ink on the documents to reveal hidden messages. Fletcher, though reluctant, provided the codes necessary to decrypt The Falcon's transmissions.

Late that night, as Grimble and Willa monitored the Whisper Web from their hangar, the intercepted message came through—a set of orders detailing a fictional mission over enemy territory.

"It's working," Fiddler whispered. "The Falcon's contacts will likely respond to this decoy, giving us a direct line to their network."

Grimble's eyes gleamed with determination. "Perfect. Let's track them and see where they lead."

Tracing the Double Agent's Network

Over the next few hours, squadron 7G monitored the decoy mission, following a series of encrypted responses that led them to the heart of the enemy's network. One by one, they identified the contacts—supply officers, communications clerks, and maintenance staff—all secretly working under The Falcon's orders.

The final signal came from a location just outside RAF Grantham, a small safehouse hidden in a cluster of trees. Willa scouted ahead, confirming that the safehouse was being used as a hub for enemy communications.

Grimble and his team moved in, surrounding the building and preparing for a confrontation. They breached the door, finding The Falcon's agents inside, each one armed but caught off guard.

"Freeze!" Willa shouted, her blaster aimed at the agents. "You're surrounded. Drop your weapons!"

The agents hesitated, then lowered their weapons, realizing they had no escape. Grimble and Fiddler quickly secured the building, confiscating documents, radios, and the encrypted messages they'd used to send orders to RAF Grantham.

The Interrogation

Back at RAF Grantham, Grimble and Ward interrogated the captured agents. Most of them were low-level operatives, unaware of the full extent of The Falcon's plan. But one of the agents finally broke, revealing the true scope of The Falcon's operation.

"The Falcon's goal was to create chaos and confusion," the agent confessed, his face pale with fear. "By issuing false orders, he could weaken your air support, sabotage missions, and create rifts among the Allied forces. He... he wanted the RAF crippled from the inside."

Grimble's expression hardened. "And where is he now?"

The agent hesitated, then muttered, "He's always moving. But last I heard, he was in London, blending in with the war offices. He's untouchable, protected by layers of disguise and subterfuge."

Grimble exchanged a grim look with Ward. "Then our mission isn't over yet."

Epilogue: A New Target

In the days following the capture of The Falcon's network, RAF Grantham returned to normal operations, though a quiet tension lingered. Squadron 7G had neutralized a major threat, but they knew The Falcon was still out there, watching, waiting for his next opportunity.

As Grimble and his team debriefed in their hidden hangar, Ward joined them, her expression resolute. "We've tracked down most of The Falcon's agents, but he's still at large. Command wants Squadron 7G to continue monitoring for any sign of him."

Grimble nodded, his voice steady. "We'll be ready. The Falcon may be clever, but he's made one crucial mistake."

Ward raised an eyebrow. "And what's that?"

Grimble's eyes gleamed with determination. "He's underestimated us."

As the sun set over RAF Grantham, Squadron 7G prepared for whatever lay ahead, knowing that the fight was far from over. They had a new target, and as long as they stood together, they would see this mission through to the end.

Section 3: The Hunt for The Falcon

RAF Grantham, Early Morning

With The Falcon's agents neutralized and their network compromised, Squadron 7G wasted no time analyzing the captured documents. The decoded messages revealed a pattern of movements leading to multiple locations across England, each site tied to intercepted RAF intelligence and sabotage efforts. All signs pointed to The Falcon himself orchestrating these activities from within London, hiding among the war offices.

Major Grimble Pebblewhisker stood at the center of the intelligence hangar, reviewing the map with his team. His sharp eyes scanned each pin and string, connecting dots across cities and towns, each marking a recent disruption or act of sabotage.

"Every lead we've uncovered points back to one thing," Grimble said, addressing his team. "The Falcon is operating within London, protected by his network. But if we can track his communications, we can flush him out."

Willa adjusted her goggles, her expression resolute. "London's a maze. He'll have plenty of places to hide. We'll need to be cautious."

Sparks, tinkering with a compact surveillance device, nodded. "If he's moving through official channels, we could catch him by monitoring restricted frequencies. I've set up this receiver to filter out non-encrypted channels and focus only on secure codes."

Fiddler leaned over the Whisper Web, tuning it to London's channels. "I'll monitor all communications coming from the city. If The Falcon's sending orders, we'll be the first to know."

Grimble gave them each a nod of approval. "Good. Pack up; we're headed to London. If The Falcon thinks he can disappear in the city, he's in for a surprise."

Arriving in London

By evening, squadron 7G had reached the bustling heart of London. The war offices were in full swing, with officers and personnel moving in and out of meetings, dispatching orders, and coordinating missions across Europe. Amid the chaos, Grimble and his team blended in, their small size allowing them to move unnoticed through the crowds of officers and staff.

The team set up a small command post in a secure corner of the underground operations bunker. Sparks' surveillance device was positioned to pick up encrypted messages within a half-mile radius, while Fiddler scanned for familiar code patterns that might match The Falcon's transmissions.

Grimble studied the war offices from a concealed vantage point, noting the flow of people and the frequency of outgoing messages. The Falcon could be anyone—an officer, a clerk, or even a messenger. They would have to watch carefully for any signs of unusual activity.

As Grimble surveyed the room, a familiar face appeared at the door: **Captain Ellie Ward**. She'd been informed of Squadron 7G's mission in London and had come to assist.

"Major Grimble," she said, stepping forward. "Command has authorized full cooperation. They've assigned me to work with you directly until we capture The Falcon."

Grimble gave her a respectful nod. "Good to have you with us, Captain. We'll need every set of eyes we can get in a place like this."

Interception of the Falcon's Message

As the night wore on, Fiddler's Whisper Web suddenly crackled to life, signaling an incoming transmission. The message was heavily encrypted, its signature matching the format used by The Falcon's network.

"Major, I've got something," Fiddler whispered, focusing on the signal. He carefully decoded the message, revealing a set of instructions marked **"Priority: Urgent"** and addressed to an unknown contact inside the war offices.

The message read: "Orders compromised at Grantham. Proceed with secondary plan. Rendezvous at Midnight—location as discussed."

Grimble's eyes narrowed. "Midnight… and no specified location. That's The Falcon all right. He's moving to execute his backup plan, whatever it is."

Captain Ward leaned in, her brow furrowing. "If he's meeting someone here, we can set up surveillance around the offices and wait for him to appear. But where would he go?"

Willa, who had been studying a map of London, pointed to an unmarked building nearby. "Look here—a storage facility attached to the war offices. It's listed as 'for repairs,' which means it's unused. Perfect place for a rendezvous."

Grimble nodded. "Excellent work, Willa. Everyone, take positions around that building. Keep out of sight, and remember—The Falcon is dangerous. No direct confrontation unless we're certain we can capture him."

Setting the Trap

With quiet precision, squadron 7G moved into position around the storage facility. Sparks rigged a few enchanted flares at key points, ready to light up the area if anyone tried to flee. Willa found a high vantage point, her miniature binoculars focused on the building's entrances, while Grimble and Captain Ward stationed themselves near the rear door, each ready to cut off any possible escape.

Midnight drew closer, and the tension thickened in the air. Fiddler relayed updates through the Whisper Web, keeping the team informed of every faint sound and movement in the building.

Then, just as the clock struck midnight, a figure emerged from the shadows—a tall man in a long coat, his face partially obscured. He moved with the practiced stealth of a seasoned operative, glancing over his shoulder before slipping into the building.

Willa's voice came through the Whisper Web. "That's him, Major. No doubt about it."

Grimble's eyes narrowed. "Hold positions. We wait until he's fully inside before we move."

Minutes passed, and then a second figure appeared—a clerk from the war offices, looking around nervously before disappearing into the building. Grimble gave the signal.

"Now," he whispered, and the team closed in.

Confrontation

Inside the building, The Falcon and his contact were deep in conversation, discussing plans to dismantle RAF operations through further forged orders. Grimble signaled for silence as he and Willa approached from behind, flanking the two men. Sparks moved to the entrance, sealing the exit with his flare trap.

Without warning, Grimble stepped forward, his voice low and steady. "It's over, Falcon. Hands up, nice and slow."

The Falcon spun around, his face flickering between shock and anger. He recognized Grimble instantly, his expression twisting with contempt. "So, you're the gnomes they sent after me," he sneered. "I thought I'd have at least another hour."

Grimble kept his weapon trained on him. "Drop the act. You've endangered lives, compromised missions, and betrayed your allies. This ends now."

The Falcon's eyes narrowed, calculating his options. "I underestimated you, I'll admit that. But you have no idea how deep this operation goes. Remove me, and another will rise to take my place. You can't win this war, Pebblewhisker."

Captain Ward stepped forward, her voice icy. "We'll see about that. Now, surrender, or we'll do this the hard way."

The Falcon smirked, but he knew he was outmaneuvered. With a resigned sigh, he raised his hands, allowing Willa and Fiddler to bind him with enchanted restraints. His contact, the clerk, cowered nearby, too terrified to resist.

Securing Evidence

With The Falcon in custody, Grimble and Ward scoured the storage facility, collecting documents, encrypted files, and even a set of forged orders ready for distribution. Every piece of evidence confirmed The Falcon's intent to destabilize Allied forces by spreading confusion and weakening air support.

"This is more than enough to expose his network," Ward said, reviewing the documents. "With this evidence, we can dismantle the remaining cells and secure our ranks."

The Falcon, bound and defiant, glared at them. "You think this will end my mission? You're fools.

There are others like me, and they won't stop until Britain is broken."

Grimble met his gaze, unflinching. "Perhaps. But as long as we stand, so does Britain. Your mission ends here, Falcon."

Return to RAF Grantham

The next morning, Squadron 7G returned to RAF Grantham, where they were met with gratitude and respect from the base staff. Word of their success had spread quickly, and the morale among the pilots and personnel was high. The forged orders had been intercepted, and The Falcon's network was in ruins.

Back at their hidden hangar, Grimble gathered his team. "Excellent work, everyone. We've cut off a major threat, but there will be more. We stay vigilant."

The team nodded, each of them proud but keenly aware of the challenges that lay ahead. They had faced one of their most dangerous enemies yet and emerged victorious. But as long as there was a war, there would be more missions.

As dawn broke over RAF Grantham, Grimble looked out at the airfield, his mind steady with purpose. Squadron 7G would continue their duty, protecting their allies from threats both seen and unseen. And as long as they stood together, no darkness could prevail.

The End.

Booklet 5

The Conspiracy of the Codebreakers: The Mission of Squadron 7G

Section 1: The Codebreaking Crisis

RAF Grantham, Codebreaking Wing, Late Afternoon, 1943

The codebreaking wing of RAF Grantham was one of the best-kept secrets of the Allied forces. It operated under strict security, with a team of specialized officers working around the clock to decode intercepted German messages and pass critical information to commanders on the front lines. Recently, however, an unsettling pattern had emerged: small, seemingly insignificant errors in the decoded messages had led to a string of costly Allied setbacks.

Major Grimble Pebblewhisker, leader of Squadron 7G, stood in a quiet corner of the codebreaking wing, watching the team of analysts as they pored over endless streams of intercepted transmissions. From his hidden vantage point, Grimble could see the intense focus on each codebreaker's face—every flicker of concentration, every sign of fatigue.

"Doesn't seem like they're slacking," Grimble murmured, half to himself, as he surveyed the room. "But those errors... they're more than simple mistakes."

Captain Ellie Ward, who had requested Grimble's help on the case, stood beside him, her expression tense. "Command can't afford any more setbacks, Major. Our missions depend on these messages, and if there's someone in there compromising them, we need to find them. Quietly."

Grimble nodded, his mind racing through the possibilities. "Understood. If there's a traitor here, they're hiding well. But my team is more than up to the task."

He gestured for his team to join him. **Willa Fernwhisk**, Squadron 7G's stealthy recon scout, slipped into position by the door. **Fiddler Twigglehook**, the communications expert, adjusted his Whisper Web to monitor nearby signals. And **Tinker "Sparks" Bogglebright**, the team's inventive engineer, prepared his tools to analyze any suspicious materials.

Grimble gave them each a nod. "Our goal is simple: find out who's tampering with these messages, and how they're doing it. If the errors aren't accidental, we need to stop them before any more missions are compromised."

Early Clues

The team split up to observe the codebreaking wing from different angles. Sparks discreetly examined some of the decoding machines, looking for signs of tampering. Willa shadowed individual codebreakers, noting their routines and any unusual behavior. Meanwhile, Grimble kept a close watch on the flow of decoded messages, tracking which hands the messages passed through before reaching Command.

An hour into the investigation, Fiddler intercepted a faint signal—a coded transmission from within the base. He quickly signaled Grimble, his expression serious.

"Major," Fiddler whispered, "I just picked up a transmission on an unauthorized frequency. Someone in this wing is sending out coded messages without clearance."

Grimble's eyes narrowed. "Whoever's responsible could be using those errors as a cover. Keep tracking that signal, Fiddler. Let's see where it leads."

Fiddler fine-tuned the Whisper Web, tracing the signal to a nearby room—the private office of **Lieutenant Charles Merrick**, a senior codebreaker known for his sharp mind and efficiency. But recently, Merrick had been tied to a few of the errors that had compromised missions.

Grimble motioned for his team to regroup. "Our first suspect is Merrick. If he's using his position to alter messages, he might be hiding more than just a few errors."

Observing Merrick

Grimble and Willa shadowed Lieutenant Merrick for the next few hours, following him as he moved between the codebreaking wing, his office, and the officers' mess. Merrick was a tall, wiry man, with a focused, calculating demeanor. He seemed to go about his work as usual, but Grimble noticed subtle signs of distraction—a glance over his shoulder, a slight hesitation as he handled certain documents.

As they followed him back to his office, Willa leaned in close, her voice barely a whisper. "He's definitely hiding something, Major. You see the way he checked his watch? Almost like he's waiting for something."

Grimble nodded. "Let's give him a little more rope. If he's waiting, we'll wait too."

Finding the Forged Errors

Meanwhile, Sparks examined the latest decoded messages in the archives, comparing them with the original intercepted transmissions. After an hour of careful analysis, he spotted a pattern in the errors: slight shifts in wording, subtle rearrangements of numbers. On the surface, they looked like minor mistakes, but when pieced together, they created delays in response times and misdirected Allied units.

"These aren't just errors, Major," Sparks said, showing Grimble his findings. "They're intentional distortions. Someone's forging these messages to delay Allied action, probably to give the Germans time to prepare countermeasures."

Grimble's expression hardened. "Then Merrick's more than just sloppy. He's actively sabotaging our efforts."

Captain Ward, who had been monitoring their findings, stepped forward. "If he's intentionally distorting the messages, that would explain why certain missions fell apart at the last moment. The Germans have been getting advance warning."

Grimble nodded, his gaze steady. "Then it's time we catch Merrick in the act. Sparks, can you set up a tracer on his equipment? We'll want to intercept any outgoing messages and see if he's in contact with a handler."

Setting the Trap

Sparks quickly got to work, discreetly attaching a tracer device to Merrick's decoding machine. The device was enchanted to track any changes Merrick made to the messages, flagging discrepancies and alerting Squadron 7G in real-time.

Later that evening, as Merrick returned to his office, the team observed from a concealed position. Merrick sat down at his desk, pulling out a set of encoded transmissions and feeding them through his decoding machine. As the messages appeared, he subtly adjusted a few words, altering coordinates and adjusting times before logging them as "decoded."

Grimble's Whisper Web buzzed to life, alerting him to the changes. "There it is. He's adjusting the message to send our forces to the wrong location," Grimble murmured.

Willa leaned in, watching intently. "And he's covering his tracks, too. He changes just enough to seem plausible."

Grimble's jaw tightened. "He's putting lives at risk with every 'correction.' Let's confront him before any more messages go out."

Confrontation

The team moved quickly, slipping into Merrick's office before he could react. Merrick froze, his hand hovering over the decoding machine as he realized he'd been caught.

"Lieutenant Merrick," Grimble said, his voice steady and unyielding. "We know you've been altering messages. Care to explain?"

Merrick's face paled, his gaze darting around the room as he searched for an escape. "I… I don't know what you're talking about. These errors are just… mistakes. I've been overworked."

Willa stepped forward, her eyes narrowed. "Mistakes don't follow a pattern, Merrick. You're forging these errors to delay Allied missions. Why?"

Merrick hesitated, his face contorting with fear and defiance. "You wouldn't understand. It's bigger than any of us."

Grimble crossed his arms, his gaze unyielding. "Try me."

After a moment, Merrick slumped, the fight draining from him. "The Germans... they found a way to contact me. Said they'd spare my family if I helped buy them time. All I had to do was delay certain messages, create small errors. No one would know."

Grimble's eyes hardened. "So you risked the lives of your fellow soldiers to protect yourself?"

Merrick looked down, his voice barely a whisper. "They left me no choice. They have agents everywhere. If I didn't comply, they would have killed me."

Grimble glanced at Captain Ward, who gave a solemn nod. They had their traitor.

Securing Evidence

With Merrick's confession, Grimble's team quickly secured his office, gathering evidence of the tampered messages and intercepting his last few transmissions. They found a set of coded signals that linked him to a network of German operatives, proving that he'd been in communication with enemy forces.

As they gathered the documents, Ward spoke quietly to Grimble. "We'll need to interrogate him thoroughly. If the Germans have agents in our codebreaking wing, they could compromise the entire Allied effort."

Grimble nodded, his voice resolute. "We'll turn every stone, Captain. Merrick's just one part of this network. The Germans may have more agents, and if they do, we'll find them."

Epilogue: Preparing for Future Threats

With Merrick's arrest, the codebreaking wing at RAF Grantham could finally operate without interference. The errors in decoded messages ceased, and the flow of accurate intelligence restored the confidence of Allied commanders.

Back in their hangar, Grimble's team gathered to debrief, each member proud of the victory but keenly aware of the stakes. They'd thwarted one spy, but the war was far from over.

Fiddler leaned back, adjusting his headset. "If Merrick was just one part of the network, who knows how many more are out there?"

Grimble's expression was firm. "We'll be ready. As long as Squadron 7G stands, we'll be a shield against every enemy plot."

As dawn broke over RAF Grantham, Squadron 7G prepared to resume their watch, knowing that new challenges lay ahead. Together, they would protect their allies from any darkness that threatened.

Section 2: Interrogation and Uncovering the Network

RAF Grantham, Interrogation Room, Early Morning

Lieutenant Charles Merrick sat in the cold, dim interrogation room, his face pale as he fidgeted with his bound hands. The traitor codebreaker glanced around nervously, knowing he was trapped. Major Grimble Pebblewhisker and Captain Ellie Ward watched him from across the table, their expressions hard and unyielding.

"Merrick," Ward began, her voice as sharp as steel, "we already know you've been tampering with messages. We need the full story. Who contacted you? How do you communicate with them?"

Merrick looked away, a sheen of sweat forming on his brow. "They… they contacted me through encrypted transmissions. At first, I thought it was just random interference, a mistake in the channels, but then the messages became… more personal. They knew everything about me. They knew how to reach me, and they knew… how to force my hand."

Grimble watched Merrick intently. "And they threatened your family. But who are they? And where are these messages coming from?"

Merrick hesitated, his voice trembling. "A contact they call 'The Viper.' He's the one in charge of the network. He uses our supply routes, intercepting deliveries from London to RAF bases. I don't know where he is exactly, but I get instructions through coded supply notes embedded in routine delivery reports."

Grimble and Ward exchanged a glance, both of them recognizing the gravity of the situation. If The Viper was using supply routes to communicate, the enemy network could be deeply entrenched, operating from within Allied logistics itself.

Gathering Intelligence

Grimble returned to Squadron 7G's hidden hangar with Merrick's confession still weighing on him. He called his team together, each member alert and ready for the next steps.

"Listen up, team," Grimble said, his tone serious. "We're dealing with a codebreaker conspiracy. Merrick has been getting orders from a contact called The Viper, using Allied supply routes as cover. If The Viper's embedded within our logistics network, he could have access to every RAF base in the region."

Willa's eyes narrowed. "So this isn't just one mole. We could be dealing with an entire network."

Grimble nodded. "Exactly. The Viper is coordinating these disruptions, and we need to find him. Fiddler, I want you monitoring every supply route. Look for irregularities in incoming and outgoing messages—anything that seems out of place."

Fiddler adjusted the Whisper Web, fine-tuning the device to pick up unusual transmissions. "Consider it done, Major. If there's an encrypted signal moving with the supply routes, I'll catch it."

Sparks grinned, reaching for his toolkit. "And I'll rig up a tracking device for the supply crates. If we can plant one in the next delivery, it might lead us straight to The Viper's hideout."

Grimble's eyes glinted with approval. "Good thinking. Let's set the trap and see who takes the bait."

Setting Up the Decoy

Using Merrick's confession as a guide, Squadron 7G devised a plan to lure The Viper out of hiding. They prepared a fake set of mission documents, embedded with information on a high-stakes Allied operation set to take place near the German front lines. The details were crafted to look enticing, a target that The Viper couldn't resist.

Sparks concealed a tracking device within the shipment, ensuring it would emit a signal only after reaching its destination. If The Viper or his agents intercepted it, Squadron 7G would be able to follow them to their base of operations.

The next morning, they sent the crate along with the routine supply convoy to a nearby base, setting the decoy in motion.

Fiddler monitored the convoy's journey through the Whisper Web, tracking every transmission and signal along the way. Hours passed, but finally, he picked up an encrypted message being sent from the convoy's route.

"Major, we've got a hit," Fiddler reported, his voice tense with excitement. "The signal just went live, and it's transmitting from a location near a coastal town. It's relaying to a secondary site further inland, most likely The Viper's hideout."

Grimble's face broke into a grin. "Excellent work, Fiddler. Let's move. We're going to catch this snake before he has a chance to strike again."

Following the Signal

Squadron 7G packed up quickly, leaving RAF Grantham under the cover of night and following the tracking signal toward the coastal town. The journey was tense, the team moving silently as they navigated through unfamiliar territory.

Willa took the lead, scouting ahead and confirming their path was clear. As they neared the signal's source, Fiddler picked up a faint transmission—coded and urgent, clearly intended to reach The Viper's inner circle.

"Major, they're exchanging coordinates," Fiddler whispered. "It's an emergency rendezvous point. They must know someone's onto them."

Grimble's eyes narrowed. "Then we don't have much time. Sparks, set up the flare traps around the perimeter. Willa, get eyes on the meeting point. We'll need every advantage if they try to run."

The team moved into position around a secluded warehouse on the outskirts of the town. Sparks placed enchanted flares along the exits, while Willa climbed to a vantage point on a nearby roof, her miniature binoculars trained on the warehouse entrance.

Just as the clock struck midnight, a dark car pulled up, and a figure stepped out—a tall man in a long coat, flanked by two other men. The team recognized him immediately: it was The Viper.

Grimble signaled his team. "That's our target. Move in, but keep it quiet. We want him alive."

The Ambush

As The Viper and his associates entered the warehouse, Squadron 7G moved into position, sealing the exits and blocking any possible escape. The Viper, noticing something amiss, turned to his men, his eyes narrowing with suspicion.

"Stay alert," he muttered. "Something's not right."

At that moment, Grimble stepped out of the shadows, his voice calm but commanding. "The game's over, Viper. You've been caught."

The Viper's eyes flashed with defiance. "Ah, the infamous gnome intelligence team. I'd heard whispers about you. Impressive, tracking me this far. But I'm afraid you're too late."

Grimble raised his blaster, his expression unyielding. "On the contrary, you've run out of time. Your network is compromised, and your agents are under arrest. Surrender now, or this ends here."

The Viper's men reached for their weapons, but Sparks activated the flare traps, flooding the room with blinding light. Caught off guard, The Viper and his associates were forced to shield their eyes, giving Squadron 7G the upper hand.

Willa swooped down from her vantage point, disarming one of The Viper's men with a swift, practiced movement. Fiddler and Sparks covered the exits, ensuring no one could escape.

Seeing his options dwindling, The Viper glared at Grimble, a smirk tugging at the corner of his mouth. "You may have caught me, Major, but my mission doesn't end here. Others will rise to continue my work."

Grimble's gaze was steady. "Perhaps. But your days of treachery are over."

Securing the Evidence

With The Viper and his associates in custody, Squadron 7G quickly searched the warehouse, uncovering a wealth of intelligence. Maps, encrypted documents, and lists of contacts—all of it confirming The Viper's role in sabotaging Allied operations.

Captain Ward, who'd been monitoring RAF Grantham, arrived to assist, her expression one of grim satisfaction as she reviewed the captured documents.

"This is it, Major," she said, looking over the files. "With this evidence, we can dismantle The Viper's network completely."

Grimble nodded; his voice was steady. "Then we'll do exactly that. We'll root out every last traitor and ensure no more lives are put at risk."

Epilogue: Return to RAF Grantham

Back at RAF Grantham, Squadron 7G was met with a hero's welcome. The Viper's capture had been a significant victory, restoring confidence and morale among the RAF personnel. The codebreaking wing resumed normal operations, with the errors and disruptions finally coming to an end.

In their hidden hangar, Grimble gathered his team, each member sharing in the sense of accomplishment.

"Outstanding work, everyone," Grimble said, pride in his voice. "We've taken down a critical threat, and the RAF can continue its work unimpeded. But we stay vigilant. There are always more challenges ahead."

The team nodded, each of them aware that while this mission was over, their duty was far from complete. They had protected their allies once again, but as long as the war raged on, Squadron 7G would be ready to stand against any threat.

As dawn broke over RAF Grantham, Grimble looked out over the base, a quiet resolve settling over him. They had faced the enemy in the shadows and prevailed—and as long as they stood together, Squadron 7G would continue to be a light against the darkness.

Section 3: The Viper's Final Words

RAF Grantham, Intelligence Interrogation Wing, Late Night

Back at RAF Grantham, The Viper sat in a secure interrogation room, bound and watched carefully by RAF guards. He exuded an eerie calm, a faint smirk playing on his lips, even as Squadron 7G and Captain Ellie Ward entered the room. It was clear that the notorious double agent felt he still had an advantage.

Grimble Pebblewhisker met The Viper's gaze, his expression steady but watchful. "You've caused enough harm, Viper. It's over. We've intercepted your orders and dismantled your network."

The Viper leaned back, chuckling softly. "Over? Major, you're only scratching the surface. My work was never just about sabotaging your missions. I'm just a single cog in a machine far greater than any of you realize."

Grimble raised an eyebrow, unfazed by The Viper's posturing. "A machine, you say? Then tell us about the next stage. What's coming?"

The Viper looked up; his eyes were cold. "An operation's underway that will render all your efforts futile. I don't need to lift a finger. It's already in motion."

Captain Ward stepped forward; her voice sharp. "What operation? Who's involved?"

The Viper smirked. "You think I'd give away such secrets? I only came here to leave you with a message—one that will echo long after I'm gone."

Grimble met Ward's gaze, then turned back to The Viper. "A message? Then deliver it, and spare us the dramatics."

The Viper's voice dropped to a whisper. "The operation is called **Red Eclipse**. And when the eclipse falls, you'll see the full power of our allies. No plane in the sky, no base on this isle will be safe."

Decoding the Final Message

With The Viper refusing to elaborate, Grimble and Ward left the interrogation room, their expressions tense as they considered his ominous words. Back in the intelligence hangar, Squadron 7G reviewed the documents captured from The Viper's hideout, searching for any mention of Red Eclipse.

Fiddler pored over a stack of intercepted messages, each one meticulously coded. "Major, if Red

Eclipse is a new operation, there should be some reference to it in The Viper's communications. It's only a matter of finding the right one."

Sparks adjusted his magnifying lens, scrutinizing a decoded message he'd been working on. "If he's using the same codes as before, I should be able to pick up any mention of an eclipse, or similar keywords."

After hours of careful work, Willa spotted a keyword embedded in one of the decoded messages—a reference to a meeting point "at the rise of the eclipse" with coordinates near a coastal airfield in Scotland. Grimble reviewed the location with a grim nod.

"Scotland… That's well within range of our defenses. If they're targeting our airbases, they'll start with our northern stations."

Ward joined them, her expression resolute. "Then we've got our next mission. Squadron 7G, I'll coordinate with the local base commanders, but this may require your team's particular expertise. If there's an infiltration network, it's likely as complex as The Viper's operation."

Grimble's eyes glinted with determination. "We're ready. If Red Eclipse is a coordinated effort to attack the RAF, then we'll dismantle it before it begins."

Securing the Northern Airbases

Over the next few days, Grimble and his team traveled to RAF Scotland's northern outposts, setting up surveillance and intercepting communications around the clock. Squadron 7G worked tirelessly, monitoring every suspicious frequency, scrutinizing every decoded message, and cross-referencing contacts on every channel.

One night, as Fiddler tuned the Whisper Web, he intercepted a faint transmission containing a string of coordinates, each one corresponding to RAF airbases across the United Kingdom. Grimble immediately flagged the message, recognizing it as part of Red Eclipse.

"Major, these coordinates… they're laying out strategic points, all Allied bases," Fiddler whispered, his voice tense. "They're preparing to strike all at once, hitting us from every angle."

Grimble's expression hardened. "Then we'll cut off their communication line. Sparks, get the disruption devices ready. Willa, find any possible staging grounds nearby. We'll intercept every operable channel before they can deploy."

Interception of Red Eclipse

The night of the supposed eclipse arrived. Grimble's team positioned themselves near a concealed airstrip, a known hotspot for covert enemy operations. As they watched, a series of vehicles approached, carrying enemy agents ready to launch the Red Eclipse operation.

Grimble signaled his team, each member poised to strike. As the agents prepared to load supplies into unmarked planes, Squadron 7G activated the disruption devices, jamming every transmission signal on the airfield.

The enemy agents, realizing they'd been compromised, scattered in panic. Grimble and his team moved swiftly, cutting off escape routes, securing the airstrip, and capturing every agent.

As dawn broke over Scotland, Squadron 7G gathered the final batch of Red Eclipse documents, securing vital intelligence on the enemy's remaining networks. Their swift action had dismantled the last phase of The Viper's operation, neutralizing a threat that could have devastated Allied air support.

Return to RAF Grantham

Back at RAF Grantham, Grimble's team debriefed with Captain Ward, who commended their courage and vigilance. "Once again, you've managed to thwart a devastating plan. Thanks to Squadron 7G, the Allied air defenses remain secure."

Grimble gave a modest nod, but his gaze was steady. "It's our duty, Captain. And we'll continue to protect our bases as long as there's a threat."

As the team gathered in their hangar, reflecting on their mission's success, Grimble reminded them of the importance of their work. "We may be small, but our role is essential. Each mission we complete brings us one step closer to victory."

With renewed purpose, squadron 7G resumed their watch, ready for whatever challenges lay ahead.

The End.

Books by Kimberley O'Dea-Grant can be found on

Amazon and Goodreads.

www.amazon.com/author/kimberleyodeagrant

Miss Chilly Mapleton Short Story Mystery Series

Tea, Scones, and Gossip in a Small Gnome Village

Halloween in Thornbrook Village

A Thanksgiving in the Gnome Village of Thornbrook

A Gnomish Christmas

WW2 Gnome Files Short Story Series

The Gnome Intelligence Unit

The Secrets of GIU Squadron 47

Tea, Scones and Discipleship

The Gnomes of Appledew Parish

Tea, Scones and Secrets Society

The New Tea, Scones and Secrets Society

Granny Spills the Beans Series

A year of Soups and Salad Dinners

A Year of Holiday Tea Parties

Other books

Delaware Cottage Cooking with Mead

Dinner Menu Planning Journal with Shopping List

Printed in Great Britain
by Amazon